California 1966.

As seen though the eyes of a German exchange student

IRENE SCHLOER

California 1966

As seen through the eyes of a German exchange student

Bibliographische Information der Deutschen Nationalbibliothek

Die Deutsche Nationalbibliothek verzeichnet diese Publikation in der Deutschen Nationalbibliografie; detaillierte bibliografische Daten sind im Internet über http://dnb.dnb.de abrufbar.

Satz, Herstellung und Verlag: BoD – Books on Demand, Norderstedt

ISBN 978-3-7407-80425

Table of Contents

Chapter 1

Through the eyes of a 17-year-old exchange student

This will be my first flight. The internationally mixed group of exchange students is boarding a plane to New York in Frankfurt. My first impression is of some grinning boys from all over the world reaching out to shake hands with everyone, looking thrilled that even girls extend their hands as well. Aside, a red-haired boy with horn-rimmed glasses, in a suit with a coat of arms on the pocket of his jacket, is demonstrating bored indifference. A few of the girls are made up.

It is left up to us to make acquaintances. Everyone speaks English. The most common opening heard is: "And where do you come from?"

All of a sudden, we become aware of the presence of a young blonde chaperone, looking happily thrilled and yelling excitedly at the top of her voice:

"Hi, everyone! (Hay?) I am Linda and I will be your guide on this flight to New York. Glad everybody is here! If you have any questions, don't hesitate to ask me at any time! You are a great group!" (How does she know?)

There is air mail paper sticking out of little plastic display boxes on the walls of the airplane. From my seat, I can see what is printed on them:

"An Bord des Lufthansafluges von ... nach ..."

After having stared at it for a few moments, I decide to take a sheet from there and write my first letter back home to my family in Heilbronn. The nice stewardess who had escorted me to my place and helped me to fasten my seat belt is passing again now and very politely asks me whether I wouldn't like to take off my overcoat. She would gladly store it in the compartment above my row. And, by the way, did I need a ball-point-pen?

In spite of her professional concern, in her uniform she reminds me rather of a policewoman or female soldier than a hostess. There are many of her kind busily rushing up and down the aisle. No man is among them. The announcements of the board loudspeakers now go on from greetings and niceties to instructions how to behave during the flight. "Remain seated" is being repeated almost obnoxiously.

I thought the plane would take off and fly right away. So I am quite surprised when it starts to juggle like a damaged car. For quite some time, we are riding on what must be a damaged plastered road. Then, all of a sudden, we stop abruptly and the engines start to roar impressively. The aircraft starts rolling much faster now, but is apparently not airborne yet.

When did we take off then? Through my loophole, I now notice in a quick sequence how the airport buildings under me are losing size, at first framed by parking lots, then disappearing altogether. Lawns, rows of houses and woods and fields are fading out of sight.

Like in the movies! But, oh no, very soon after, nothing is visible but fog. Even the sky is hidden behind it.

But when we finally are flying over sunlit clouds, I think how nice it should be to ride on one of these now. I know they would hold tight; I can tell by their solidly packed shapes. And if not, there are countless others floating under them that would catch me, if I dropped down.

I hear my fellow passengers cheer with pleasure as the swinging begins. Some have unfastened their seat belts and have got up, running back and forth in the center aisle. A strict announcement in German and English makes them dart back. The stewardesses serve tea. But why are there still ice cubes in it, even though it is quite cold?

Another announcement tells us that the topping on the appetizers is veal, not pork. Who cares! However, there are audible approving grunts coming from some of the seats. I am busy enjoying my snack: besides the veal roll there is also an asparagus sandwich with mayonnaise. As a desert, we are served an appetizing-looking strawberry pie with cream and then coffee. The metal cutlery is wrapped up in a napkin; sugar, salt, pepper and milk are placed in small packages on the serving tray. I put the pepper in my handbag and decide to include it in my first letter home.

After a short stopover in Shannon, Ireland, the aircraft leaves the continent. Although the wing under my window is impairing my view, I can still see a lot. And there are constant announcements telling us where we are and what there is to see. I can't believe how narrow the Channel is! I recognize the chalky rocks on the coast of Dover, I have been there before. From above, they look so unspectacular. Gradually, looking outside becomes boing. And isn't it quite late? It just doesn't get dark. For hours, there is nothing to see but heaps of whipped cream outside. The next announcement, though, wakes all of us up. The skyline of New York is coming into sight! Not yet, not yet, but then…Tension is released among cries of joy.

"Do you carry any food? Salami?" a customs officer asks me putting his hand into my carry-on bag without being bashful about it. Outside, Gerdie is waiting.

"Hi, I'm your chaperone!"

She gets on a bus together with all the girls. We are heading for our hotel, where I will share a large room with four other girls. We see two high-rising king-size beds with an extra portable bed at the foot-end of one of them. The four other girls turn out to be Turkish, all of them speaking fluent English, except when talking to each other, of course.

"Where do you want to sleep?" Shermin asks me politely.

I take the extra bed which is quite all right for one person, as I find. What a luxury! Our room has a bathroom all for itself. The shower head is mounted firmly into the tile wall instead of hanging over the tabs. My roommates have already turned on the TV set and heated water in a cooker on the side table. Now they are scrutinizing the manual of the telephone in order to find out how much an external call would cost. Two of the girls smoke. We are expected to come to dinner at a place which is described elaborately in our instructions. They speak about a 15-minutes' walk through the skyscraper world of Manhattan. It turns out to be a scary experience. Not that the streets are as narrow as it seems at first glance, but the buildings are so high that the impression they make is almost threatening.

We lose our way. Instead of walking straight ahead crossing six streets and then turning left into one of the avenues, we miss the correct turn. To our great relief, there is another group of AFSers at the crossing, also looking for the cafeteria.

Back in the hotel room, I start to wash myself over the wash basin with my wash-rag I brought with me. Like I am used to, I am rubbing my armpits, when I notice one of my Turkish roommates looking on with an expression of disgust on her face.

"You are not going to see your host family like this, are you? Do you want to borrow my razor?"

Feeling offended, I answer back snottily. Pulling up her diligently plucked eyebrows, she leaves the bathroom.

We stay at The Shelburne for three nights. In the first one, there is already trouble. The Turkish girls are fighting loudly about something which must have to do with the climate, because I only understand the word "Klima" being repeated.

Slowly, it is getting warmer in the room. The rubber curtains aren't helping the flow of fresh air, either. I throw off my covers and still can't sleep all night.

Chapter 2

You are in LA now

At Los Angeles airport, a stocky woman with kind of a cauliflower hairstyle and red nail polish on is storming towards me and loudly informs me:

"Ayriin, I'm your mom!"

I look at her with relief and happiness and I stammer: "Glad to meet you!"

Behind her at a reasonable distance comes a lanky man with glasses on, at least one foot taller than her. A curly-haired teenager in a floral cotton dress is hiding behind him, holding a short, straw-blonde girl of preschool-age by the hand.

"Don. Kim. Steph. "

We are heading towards a big car. We youngsters have more than enough space in the back seat. The car has fenders that look like the sleeves of an angel. It is of blue and white color.

Yes, they had sent me photos of their family and I recognize them now. A cold can of Coke is put into my hand and I watch Kim opening hers and then skillfully sipping it. While driving, mind you.

We quickly get to Azusa via broad highways and I watch my new dad lift my heavy suitcase out of the trunk and drag it into Kimberly's room. There are two beds and a breached plastic folding screen camouflaging them. On one wall of the room there is a large sliding door that opens a closet.

Through the vertically arranged window, which is being closed by a sliding upper part and a window catch, I can see a large swimming pool in the backyard. I involuntarily take a deep breath, impressed. Yes, there is a palm tree there too. Around it there is a concrete wall with an orange tree and a hibiscus hedge hiding it. The grass is yellow, but the hedge is bursting out in bloom.

The next morning already, we are on the road again - heading for a cottage by a lake in the mountains. The lake is crystal clear, dark blue and proves not to be too cold. Around it there are fir trees, tall and slim, not standing very close. The soil looks dry. There are funny signs with pictures everywhere: Smokey the Bear helps to prevent forest fires.

As good as it feels paddling and swimming all day, in the evening I have a terrible sunburn, blistered feet and, on top of it all, diarrhea. Feeling miserable, I let myself fall down in a rocking chair on the porch and start crying.

The family tactfully overlooks it. I am trying to make them out; Mom is always at ease; Kimberly is very conscientious and Stephanie is spoiled. Dad is an artist; I have already noticed his pictures hanging everywhere in the house in Azusa. The garage is his studio.

Kim now carefully sets out to sprinkle flour on my back and thighs and Mom gives me two aspirins. I sink into my bed and decide to watch out better what I am doing from now on.

The next morning I'm actually much better, but the sunburn still hurts terribly. I am not supposed to go outside on this day and instead I take notice of my surroundings for the first time. We are in a log cabin, even the beds are made of tree trunks. But there is electricity, running water, a stove and a fridge in the kitchen as well as a TV in the family room and a washing machine and dryer in a sort of crate in the back the house. The bathroom, where there is a shower, sink and toilet, is equipped with laminated walls and floor. Above all, comfort is taken care of.

We are in a "share cabin", a holiday home for many families, who are all entitled to a certain number of days of stay per year. Because I am not allowed to go out, I come up with the craziest ideas, for example I looking for a vacuum cleaner and starting cleaning.

In the kitchen there is delicious food, brought by mom. The Americans heat up cooked ham as thick as a steak, while in Europe we would eat it in thin slices on a sandwich. There are boiled corn cobs, which are eaten with butter spread on and sprinkled with salt. They just taste delicious. Chopped-up sweet and sour cucumbers ("relish") complete the meal. For dessert, we eat rich ice cream with chocolate sauce on top, which is poured hot onto the scoops and immediately freezes solid. In addition, we have unbelievably delicious tasting watermelon, which can also be eaten as a snack, and at any time people of the day, we can have potato chips and coke.

Life can be so wonderful! Meanwhile, Kimberly is familiarizing me with the local dangers. Rattlesnakes should be avoided, if possible, you can hear them from a distance. It is more like the sound of a children's rattle than that of a clatter and also in no way comparable to the insisting chirping of the crickets that I heard in the garden of our Azusa house.

The mosquitos are very annoying, though, and hardly anyone is being spared. At night you can lower the mosquito nets from the ceiling if things become unbearable. I look up and wave my thanks when I see the dust.

Chapter 3

Pool Parties

My mother has written me a letter. A message from home!

After having read it over and over, a selfish though occurs to me: If her letters arrived, parcels would do the same, wouldn't they. So, I write to her, I need my bathing cap and special soap and a few nice presents for Steph.

The party which Kim throws for our classmates shortly before school starts, is really stunning. I had never experienced anything like that before.

The music is loud and inviting. For a while I watch the girls in bikinis with floral patterns move rhythmically and the boys hanging around, wearing knee-length pants, which they also leave on when swimming (!).

Very soon, everyone begins to dance. Arms are thrown up one by one. Their legs seem either to jump from front to back or from right to left. They sometimes also just stand still and only their hips move while the head keeps nodding up and down.

I ask Kim: "What is the name of that dance?"

She gives me a wide grin: "They call it The Monkey. But really everybody does what they want."

There is a queue at a grill on the lawn. On a small table next to it there are paper plates, napkins and two giant bottles with a pumping device: ketchup and mustard. Everyone is getting themselves sausages, hamburgers and kind of rubbery bread rolls. Countless cans of cola are spread out on ice cubes in a giant open beach bag.

Could Dad please toast my strange bun on the grill?

"Sure. Here you go! "

I slowly start to relax, increasingly enjoying the ambiance.

The girls are all made up and their legs and armpits are shaved. They are obviously trying to stay away from the water. I quickly find out where this aversion is coming from. Again and again, two or three boys grab a girl and throw her into the pool with a howling, cheered by the whole crowd.

Everyone looks tanned and seems to be in a good mood. The most common word I hear is "fun".

"Isn't it fun ?!" - "I'm having so much fun! "-" Yeah! " - "Yeah bow!"

Clothing, I soon notice, is an important issue in people's lives. A woman or a young girl at school or at work needs to wear something different and freshly cleaned every day. Men wear a kind of uniform which they change every day, though. I am amazed by the many identical shirts, T-shirts, sneakers etc. that are part of a man's outfit. A man often buys himself the same items over and over again or in multiple numbers. An absolute must-have seems to be button-down shirts in white or light blue with high neck undershirts with short sleeves underneath. Even their sweaters and suits are very much alike. Ties usually have diagonal stripes in three subdued colors on them.

In their free time, men wear Bermuda shorts with belts and colored T-shirts. These signal their belonging to a sports or other club, the same is true for their jackets. Zipped "lettermen" jackets have sewn-on symbols that immediately signal to the knowing where these young people belong to. Sweaters are dark blue or mottled brown and often sport a cable pattern. A lot of men and boys wear baseball caps in their free time. Shoes to match are moccasins or sneakers. At work everyone has on the same type of leather shoes with an edging displaying perforated patterns.

During all my year in the United States, I have never seen an unshaven man.

These well-groomed young people at my first pool party are behaving in a compliant manner, as they usually do, I found out. Long conversations between two persons are almost a no-go.

Party talk is done in rapid succession and rather superficially about common things like school, which is going to start in a few days. Who are you supposed to be taking math from? Certainly, there will be new teachers. But as a "Senior" you can choose almost all courses yourself.

The focus seems to be on the "extra-curricular activities". Most of the boys want to be part of a "varsity team" in sports, meaning two hours of extra training in the afternoon – every day.

From what I catch, they are now talking about me.

"Her English is good, but her accent is so funny!"

"Are you kidding? I love it. It is so European!"

"She *is* from Europe, you blockhead!"

"She is pretty, except for her face ..."

"You think so? She reminds me a little of Kim Novak."

"Shhh-ure. She is a brunette!"

Slowly I begin to get irritated when someone in my presence speaks of me in the third person. I decide to respond and that proves successful. I start talking to Kathy, Peggy and Cherie. Kim looks on, apparently pleased. "Good show"! she seems to think, encouragingly.

I hear two boys whispering behind us.

"Why don't you call her up and ask her for a dee ay tee ee?" Triumphant giggle is following: " I knew she wouldn't get it if I spelt it! "

After everyone has gone, Kimberly explains to me everything about dating customs in a long monologue. Everything looks informal, but it really has a strict framework.

If a boy is interested in a girl, he calls her up and asks her out to the cinema or even just for a coke. Invitations from person to person are taboo. If he walks with the same girl a couple of times, they "go" together. If they are then seen together frequently, they "go steady". High school students then often swap their school rings, he wears hers on his little finger, she wraps a string around the narrow end of his ring and proudly presents it on the ring finger of her right hand. This may result in a marriage proposal or else in a tragic end, which must then be made clear to everyone.

I'm confused. And if you don't go to the beach with one person but with several, for example?

Kim gives me a broad smile:

"That's very nice! No sex. We call it group dating."

I also need to know a few important facts, she explains to me patiently and clearly. She would make a good teacher.

So there seem to be various dance events at school, which often take place in the gym, but you have to dress up properly, the boys wear black trousers and a white jacket, the girls long evening dresses. The girl goes to these events with the boy who calls and asks her first. Even if she was invited shortly afterwards by someone else she liked better (could happen, couldn't it?), a decent girl unfortunately had to refuse. However, she was allowed to drop a hint like she had already been asked.

My foster sister looks at me as if she has read my thoughts, because she hurries to explain that cheating and lying were not allowed at all, because in no time the whole school would know who had invited whom.

I am almost overwhelmed by this amount of information, but it gets even better. When you kiss, especially when you say goodbye, it's accepted, Kimberly states with a wink of her eye. And if you smooch in the car, which no decent girl will do on her first date, you call it "necking".

Automobile? Do 16- or 17-year-olds drive a car? Apparently, they do, and the police are chasing parked cars at night. They only fine people who have taken off something, even their shoes. It is immoral, against the ruling customs and is therefore prohibited. This is why many young people smooch in the open-air cinema, where the police don't look and everyone is busy with themselves.

So, where were we? Necking? The next step is the "making out". That would lead to pregnancy and you would have to get married or give the baby away for adoption.

I feet exhausted and taken aback. Gosh! I have a favor to ask.

"If it is convenient, could we some time go swimming to the beach together with a few others?"

We are not going to the sea for some time to come, but Kim has a great surprise waiting for me before school starts.

It is the Beatles America concert in the Rose Bowl, which I am privileged to watch live on August 30, 1965, two weeks after my arrival in California. Kim and some of her friends are taking me with them.

Three of us are in the back seat, giggling, Kim is at the wheel. Seat belts are not yet widely used.

There is a sort of huddle at the entrances to this modern amphitheater, but there are a lot of directions and barriers and the potential visitors are generally well-mannered. Warning signs blare out at us everywhere: No bottles, no food, no high-heeled shoes, no change of seat, etc. There are marshals, paramedics and guides. The feeling of being on the secure side is also being reaffirmed by the availability of plenty of information pointing out emergency exits and toilets (!) The excitement of people in high spirits is felt all over the open-air theater. The thrilling voice of the animator reaches every visitor by loudspeakers in all directions, making the audience almost horny for what is coming up.

The instruments are already set up on the stage. Although we are sitting quite far up in the rear, we immediately recognize each of the adored four from Liverpool upon their spectacular entry.

The shouting comes suddenly and is therefore all the more overwhelming.

"Paul!" "George!" "Ringo!" "John!"

"Joooohn, Pauauauaul. John!"

"Paul" I hear myself yelling in spite of myself.

The mushroom heads in their good suits wave and bow, and then the concert starts. Well, whatever next? Their entrance song is "Twist and Shout"!

There is unabashed singing along, clapping along, coming almost naturally. The girls are red in the face, tears are rolling down their cheeks.

Everyone is screaming at the top of their lungs when the final chord is fading away.

"A Hard Day's Night!"

One song follows the other, the Fab Four also present contemplative melodies like "She's a Woman".

"Ticket to Ride, Ticket to Ride, Ticket to Ride" comes a request from the ranks, first tentatively, then rhythmically. "

"You guys're going to have to wait for that one." That was Ringo.

"Can't buy me love!"

"I'll buy you a diamond ring, my friend, if it makes you feel alright. I'll get you anything my friend, if it makes you feel alright. But I don't care too much for money. Money can't buy me love…

They hit the nerve of the times: rebellion against uninhibited capitalism and demand for the return to love of one's neighbor; which is admittedly utopia, the realization of which then seemed possible for many years to come.

It is impossible not to be carried away by the prevailing emotions. Whatever Paul had asked of us, we surely would have sobbed "Yes, we will" altogether.

At the end of the concert, we start looking for our car, totally distraught. Kim is the only one to have kept a (relatively) sound mind and to remember roughly where the car was.

It takes an hour for us to hit the highway. This is partly due to the fact that we are spending a lot of time in line in front of the drive-in, because we are hungry and, above all, thirsty.

It's really impressive how Kim is taking every single one of us safely home.

Chapter 4

High School

Kim and I walk to school, for the first time not on the day lessons start, but in the week before school reopens after a long summer holiday. It is registration day. This means we are getting in line, getting in line again and again and three times again. This takes us about five-and-a half hours: We are registering for the final class in secondary education, class 12, called Seniors. We fill in different form, have our pictures taken, get our books, show our vaccination certificates and talk with old classmates.

Newspaper people are present as well, interviewing and photographing for local papers and radio stations. The Seniors are visibly enjoying their status.

According to state laws, every student is supposed to go through 12 years of schooling and get a high school diploma. On the other hand, there is no legal obligation to attend school after the age of 16. Not all teenagers manage to hang on till the end. They are stigmatized as "Drop-outs".

There are lots of incentives to lure the students into staying on till graduation. School is taking up the greater part of the youngsters' daily routine. Although everybody takes about 5 to 7 courses per day, almost nobody is finished before 4 pm. There are countless afternoon activities which are almost obligatory to attend. Every student has her personal advisor who suggests a schedule of required and extra-curricular courses.

Whatever the youngsters' interests, they can choose between music, arts, sports and social clubs of many levels. These clubs are not the same as e.g., European workshops, but practically no different from regular school. Every day, in sports, for example, there is very competitive hard training, the choirs practice diligently for their next concerts, the theater clubs rehearse inevitably for performance.

The variety of clubs offered is amazing. Not only are different levels of difficulty available, but also of sophistication. These clubs can be attended by students of all four years of secondary education, meaning talented and interested Freshmen (9th grade) can be in a group with 12th graders as well.

I myself decide to participate in a girls' choir.

The most prestigious club seems to be the one with the yearbook editors. At the end of their Senior year, every class presents a quite voluminous issue of their life at school with all there was to it. Though they, of course, do dominate the book, there are also pictures of undergraduates and teachers and staff.

The students' schedule is arranged really practically. Every student has the same chosen courses at the same time every day, five days a week. For me, this means: 1st period Maths, 2nd period Literature and Composition, 3rd Period Spanish, 4th period French, 5th period Government, 6th period Sports. After two weeks of lessons, I swap Maths for Home and Family.

But it is not only lessons and clubs that attach the students to their school, strengthening also their personality and inducing them to improve their performance.

Every morning before lessons start, all students assemble for unisono pledging allegiance to their flag, putting their right hands to their hearts and looking up at the American flag. Immediately following, they sing together the individual school hymn, in our case, Azusa High School. As soon as it is over, everybody claps their hands and jeers.

Well, I am free to participate actively or not, according to my own will and choice. They suggest, I don 't say aloud the Pledge of Allegiance or sing the National Anthem, but just listen respectfully. The United States of America are agreed to be the best country in the world, but in spite of this, I should not betray my own country because of this fact. The school hymn was mine also, certainly, and I was expected to sing along fully hearted. This was to be true especially for Saturday evening football games or other interschool competitive events in the stadium.

More and more I come to realize that being a student in California is a full-time job, in which even the weekends are meaningfully embedded. And when my foster sister Kim tells me about guided summer holiday camps for students, I come to realize the big difference between the German and the American school systems.

My education in post-war Germany seems noncommittal in comparison. My teachers in Heilbronn did not try hard to shape my identity, it seems to me now. And as to performance, yes, there is an incentive to be good in classes and to learn a lot, but the American way of rewarding every single manifestation of progress or success is completely new for me.

The American way of education induces the will to belong to the best, no matter whether in sports, grade point average or even smart looks. The respective "winners" are rewarded and show their pride unabashedly, even if only nominated for "Christmas Queen". With one event preceding the next, the whole school year is full of special balls, which begin quite early after classes start with the "Homecoming Dance".

Marching proudly ever forward

To victory and to fame

Azusa High, our Alma Mater,

Glorious be thy name.

Through the years our hearts will cherish

Times we've spent with you.

Memories will never perish.

We're forever true.

I am a little shocked as well as bewildered. Trying to remain honest and fair, I explain to my teachers and fellow students that in Germany we have neither a pledge to the flag nor is the national anthem ever played or sung in school. Nobody is being proud of their own school or thinks it be better or worse than others. Our school teams, if there are any, don 't play other schools in the big stadium on Saturdays either.

My truly intelligent sister frowns at that.

"That's not Communism, no. It must be Socialism. And Americans think the Germans are Nazis."

This really knocks me off. Never ever had anyone connected me personally with Nazis. After all, I was born three years after the end of the Hitler regime.

At that time, I still had no idea that similar comparisons would upset me again and again, later in life.

Chapter 5

Aztecs and other Mexicans

They like to stay among their kind, Kim assures me. In the beginning, I recognize them by their smartly done excessive hairdos and also by their faces which feature a rather reserved expression. The girls' hair is rattled very high, the boys have shiny, fixed hair. Their names are Jose Lopez, Isabela Sanchez, Sergio Venezuela. In the Sixties, Rosemary Gomez und John Rodrigez are still in the minority of their likes.

They live in their own neighborhoods, and if a Mexican family buys a home in a middle-class part of town and moves there, the value of the other homes invariably decreases. The Leitners, Robertsons, McDouglases, Clarks and Petries then one by one sell their houses and move away.

California was Spanish speaking and Mexican, even for a long time after 1848, when the victory of the American troops over the Mexican ones resulted in the new states of Texas, California, Arizona, Nevada, Utah and parts of New Mexico, Colorado and Wyoming. The original names of regions and settlements were kept and the educated migrants coming out west continued to pronounce them the way they sound in Spanish. Still, the obligatory accent of the American speaker leaves no doubt as to their loyalty:

"La Hoya (La Jolla) ", "Pesadeena (Pasadena)" and "Sanhosey (San Jose)" took me some time to identify at first. Certainly, there have been also changes of names or adaptations, especially for the bigger settlements. Frisco replaced San Francisco, LA was soon used instead of Ciudad de los Angeles; Anaheim, Long Beach or Oakland are examples of new names.

The population of California is growing constantly. Many new immigrants are still seeking their luck in the "Golden State". They have lots of room where what had originally been orange groves are being cleared. At first it was the lure of gold which attracted migrants to move to California. Gold was supposed to be abundant in the rivers like Sacramento.

Later, liberal California (outlaw California?) promised unlimited freedom. The eastern states had slowly become established and enforced many more restrictions (laws) than the West had. In between the world wars, the film industry with many European directors included moved to southern California, and not only because of the mild climate there. They soon founded the movie town "Hollywood".

The legend went on and by and by scientists were attracted by salaries and conditions in newly founded private universities like Stanford. Soon, Silicon Valley near San Francisco was born. Incidentally, the beginnings of the computer industry and digital times can be loosely connected to the late Sixties, the time I spent a year as an exchange student in Azusa.

Coming to speak of the Aztecs whom Azusa High School identified with and all of our sports teams were named after, yes, they once did live in that region. Now the new inhabitants saw their common roots in the Aztecs and considered themselves their proud descendants. In this way, one could cleverly dissociate oneself from the Spanish conquistadores of the 16th and 17th centuries. The language of the different Aztec tribes and their kings and gods allowed for colorful names to give for example to the Seniors of southern Californian schools which adorned their corresponding year books.

Even the phantasy dresses of the cheer leaders and the uniform sports outfits were designed with the corresponding Aztec tradition in mind. By the way, the well-built indigenous drummer of our Marching Band in all the splendor of his feathered outfit really resembles the stereotype Aztec in our minds.

The colors of our school are exclusively limited to royal blue, white and black. The motto of all schools seems to be: Your school, your colors, your home.

So, what about the true descendants of the Mexicans who have to make it in these schools? When I was a student there in the 1960ties, they seemed to me to be underrepresented in for example all afternoon activities Their best bet seemed to be excelling in sports.

Boys and girls have separate sports lessons. After every lesson, they have to take a quick shower and then show their wet towels as a proof to their teachers. These mark in their grade books who showered and who didn 't. This fact is responsible for another obvious clash of new immigrant

American and traditional Mexican cultures, because Mexican girls from the south hesitate to show themselves without dress to anyone else, no matter what gender.

However, the Ministry of Education signals zero tolerance: to be an American means to adhere to American customs. And Americans see nothing wrong in being naked in front of peers of the same sex if the occasion and mutual activities ask for it. This goes for a large part of Europeans as well.

American teachers are always available for parents' consultations, of course.

"Listen, Mrs. Pascal, my daughter is not going to undress in front of others."

"And why is that, Mrs. Gomez?"

"We are not brought up that way."

"Then maybe you should go and live where your daughter doesn't need to conform to American rules."

As for the prestige clubs at school like "Government", where the American government is being reincarnated in miniature, meaning you have a president, a vice president and many other authentic administrative functions, there are no Spanish names found.

What about other minorities? As late as 1964 blacks in the United States were granted the same rights as whites, so called WASPs (white Anglo-Saxon Protestant). John F. Kennedy was the first American president to not have been a Protestant. When he was elected in 1961, the talk of the town was his Irish (Catholic) background. But "The Winds of Change" were blowing ever more forcefully, until at the end of the Sixties a real revolution of values and attitudes took place.

In 1966, actors of Hollywood were already stirring up public conscience with their protest songs and young people took over their ideas quite readily. Joan Baez, Cher, Bob Dylan, partly also The Beatles, The Rolling Stones and many others became idols and found more and more followers.

In the realm of fashion, skirts became an inch shorter, girls stopped wearing figure shaping bras, nylons and leather shoes with high heels. This was true in part also for freaky Orange County, part of which was Azusa. All of a sudden teenagers became aware of being supervised and guided in their sexual behavior, just for the purpose of securing increase in population. The cheeky ones turned topsy turvy, claiming they had tried group sex and marihuana, called pot. All this was then just barely noticeable, nevertheless, it was a real trend that was to last for some time to come.

Chapter 6

School is our Life

My first test results:

Lit&Comp   B

US Govt   B

French   B-

My teachers seem satisfied with these grades, and Kim is, too. As to her own grades, she seems to be more ambitious, studying all the time to get a straight A grade average. College will be expensive, even a state university like for example UCLA will strain any family budget. Besides, not all colleges are of the same quality, it is agreed. Some do have a good reputation, ane even the ones that don 't, are free to refuse any applicant. Students with a very good grade point average have to present a record of social and sports activities as well, if they want to get accepted at a prestigious university which, in turn, is as good as a top job guarantee.

Of course, it also helps to present a few letters of recommendation from renowned professors and other teachers.

In order to get excellent grades, students are in the habit of researching constantly, mostly at libraries, since broad knowledge cannot be obtained from school books and lectures only.

At High School level, students have to draw up their own presentations. Those, in turn, must contain verifiable footnotes. This means, getting down to researching independently in the library and run your fingers through index card boxes. The "Dewey Decimal System", according to which libraries arrange their books, is easy to master and interesting to test. Moreover, when the presentation is all ready, one gets extra points for adding polaroid photos or articles cut out from magazines.

On Saturdays and Sundays, though, there is supposed to be no homework or studying. Sunday morning is reserved for church, Saturday is dating day or party. Dating can be quite relaxed and non-binding, like a group of people, fellow students or interest groups (here AFS comes in heavily) getting together. A date between a girl and a boy, though, has its rules like going to the movies or having a candlelight dinner at a restaurant. More often than not, Saturday night is reserved for interschool games, especially American football.

I have already been to my first football game. Two rivalling school from different communities played each other, with practically the whole schools watching, students, teachers and families. Everybody sports their own colors, wearing sports outfits, lettermen jackets, T-shirts with prints showing their loyalty or at least where they belong. The players are more like fighters and wearing protective gear over their heads and faces as well as over their elbows and knees. The ball is not round, but rather egg-shaped.

This type of game has nothing to do with European football and little with English rugby. There are two goals at the end of either half of the lawn. The maximum 11 members of each team allowed on the lawn at one time (there are a lot more around) are either defense or attack players. They hang on tightly to their ball and start to run to place it somehow on the field of the opponent team. This, of course, is the last thing those in turn would let happen. So, they crowd around the attacker and make him somehow let go off it. They jump, burst and dive into each other and this continues throughout the whole game.

The fans of each team get more and more exited and also their part of exercise, since they jump up and down, their arms flying in the air. Thousand voices become one and it is impossible not to be influenced by the atmosphere. According to the cheerleaders, the fans shout slogans, make appropriate noises, jeer and applaud. If their luck changes, they can also be deadly quiet, or grunt or cry. Like collective hysteria, the wave of emotions touches everyone. All of a sudden it comes to my mind, that students and fans must feel terribly lost when they move house. Or is it rather like the saying goes: The king is dead, long live the king?

Azusa wins the first game of the season by beating Glendora, their arch rival, the richer, more sophisticated neighbor town. At the end of the game, joy has no limits. The pompom girls cry with relief, though being careful not to spoil their make-up. Again and again, they swing their legs and shake their pompoms toward the crowd. The pompoms are like huge mops made of paper or plastic bands tied together on one end. For Azusa, they are either white or royal blue, as you can easily guess.

With so many new impressions, almost all exchange students are overwhelmed. AFS knows this well and has many volunteer members who take care of the youngsters, prepare and coach them as to what they should expect. Every AFSer has a special personal advisor she can always call. Besides, there are regular get-togethers, meetings where all AFSers of one region are hosted at private parties, usually at a house of the wealthier volunteers around a swimming pool.

My advisor Mr. Kayman and his wife give me some stamps as a present and ask what else I need. I would like some deodorant, so I won't have to borrow my foster sister's all the time. I first refuse the stamps as a gift, but the Kayman's say, it would be my birthday soon, anyway.

A few days later I receive a letter from "your uncle George" with a check in it. It says 20 Dollars on it. My mother had written to an old friend from her school days now living in Ohio, whom she had kept in contact with. She had explained in her letter that I had asked her for a deodorant, whatever that was.

Mom Lorraine and I go to a bank where I show my passport and sign a receipt. Since I sign my name as "Irene Schlör" and not "Irene Schloer", the way it was written on the check, the bank won't accept it. After long and elaborate explanations, the clerk got tired of me and conceded to pay out the amount if I did sign it again:

"But exactly the way it is written on the check!"

In every aspect, the AFS chapter, its president and its volunteers are very considerate of my needs and never let me down with anything, however trifle. When, at the first get-together, Mrs. Robertson gives us hand-outs to fill in, my attention is caught by the item "What I miss". I spontaneously write "Coffee". The next day in the afternoon, the doorbell rings and Mrs. Robertson comes in with a cooking pot with a filter device and a pound of ground coffee to go with it. I am so thankful that I become emotional. How nice they all are!

Talking about food and drink, for breakfast Americans have a very light coffee, mostly the instant version. If you take a big helping of it to wake you up, it tasses very bitter. Aside of it, you usually eat a bowl of corn flakes or other dried and roasted cereal with milk. There are countless sorts of it, with honey, with chocolate, with nuts added. Milk is sold in tetra packs in gallons (approximately four liters) or quarts.

I like most of the food very much. I even start gaining weight. My new favorites are besides grapefruit, avocados. I can't believe that people don't pick them up when they lie in their front yards or alongside some streets, ripe and fallen to the ground. If you cut them vertically and take out the big seed, they are ready to eat right away! Just squeeze some grapefruit juice over the halves and sprinkle salt and pepper on them. With a slice of toasted bread, you have a delicious snack. Guacamole is another dish I can't get enough of.

At noon, the students eat in the school's cafeteria. Mom gives us each 50 cents every morning for that purpose only. Kim and I get us a sandwich each. Some of the girls, worrying about staying slim, take only some salad with no dressing on it. Of course, they get hungry. Then they chew gum. Some of them eat and afterwards run to the toilet to throw up their lunch. That is what they call their secret of staying super slim.

There are also students who bring food from home, mostly fruit. After school, they have tacos, burritos or tortillas at one of the many fast-food chains featuring Mexican food. Food chains like McDonald's or Pizza Hut are rather places to go to for dinner.

Personally, I don't care much for corn flour, so I stick to "Chili con carne", beans with meat, when I am at a Mexican place. I learn how to love and fear hot peppers.

Europeans get sentimental when talking about American ice cream variations, and they are absolutely right. Ice cream is sold in huge containers and kept in the freezing department of the fridge. There are, no exaggeration, a thousand flavors of it. Kids and teens eat it with big spoons, while sitting in their rooms on their beds doing homework. The radio is usually on, blasting lively hits. This seems to help them concentrate. Every teen has her favorite radio station with its own recognition signal and its name sung. Between the songs featured, there are commercials and short comments thrown in. After all this time, my ears are still ringing with "K.R.L.A. – encore, encore!" and "K.F.W.B. – 98!"

In the evening, people usually have their main meal at home. My foster mom is a good cook, more often than not we have casserole dishes like Lasagna. Sometimes Dad is grilling hamburgers in the backyard around the pool. The electrical grill needs no charcoal and can be stored where it is used.

After dinner, Mom Lorraine sometimes will sit in front of the TV and zap back and forth between programs. She usually has a big bowl of popcorn on her lap. On the other hand, Kim and I almost never watch TV. From now and then, though, the whole family gathers in the living room in front of the TV and we have roasted marshmallows.

If we get hungry at night, the accepted thing to do is to make ourselves a peanut butter-and -jelly sandwich. It is very rich and nutritious, so no pangs of hunger for the rest of the night are guaranteed.

If you go out, you usually have steak. When ordering, you have to say how you want it prepared. If you don't like blood on your plate, you order it "well done". The most common alternative to steak is chicken. Logically enough, this is being offered at a chicken place, not at the steak place. They have chicken in many variations, grilled or fried, as a soup or baked or plain cooked. I love the grilled variation with pineapple and cantaloupe (nothing against cranberries or boysenberries either).

Having dessert at a restaurant is not a typically American tradition. Afternoon coffee and cake gatherings are, in turn, not the custom. If you happen to have a sweet tooth, you frequent the bakery and get something to take out. You get the items wrapped and arranged in paper boxes. Your best choices are mini cakes filled with chocolate or nuts (muffins), or dough made with yeast in the form of a ring and coated with sugar or icings (bagels or donuts).

To go out to eat, you can also go to an ice-cream parlor. This means, dessert is your main meal. My favorite is Hot Fudge Sundaes (a guaranteed

1000 calories per helping). This means a few huge scoops of vanilla ice-cream mixed with walnuts or pecans, toppled with hot chocolate sauce, on top of which in turn is sprayed a generous amount of whipped cream and this is crowned with a sugared cherry.

The hip thing to do is going out for breakfast. There is a buffet with fruit, cheese and marmalade.

Aside from these, you order your main dish, which is an egg or two in countless variations: omelets with bacon or vegetables, scrambled egg with shrimp, sunny side up or boiled. Some people have creamy porridge which is very filling or pancakes with maple syrup, of which you shouldn't have too many, either. You toast your own slices of bread as desired and have a feast, a meal to last you all day.

Chapter 7

Family

I am crazy after mail from home. This is slowly starting to get on the nerves of my host family. Actually, most of the time, Dad is in his studio in the garage, painting. Mom is usually out at her job when Kim and I get home in the afternoon. Steph loves to rebuke us with wise remarks she has picked up somewhere. Well, 5-year-olds and 16-year-olds usually don't match.

Dad carefully paints my name on my gym clothes and he doesn't even need a stencil to do it. It looks cool. Since all students have the same uniform outfits for PE – a short-sleeved white blouse with snap fasteners and black shorts to go with it - we need to have our names on them.

Dad also gets busy with the pool, its pumps and cleaning. He has different sticks with nets on them which he uses to fish diligently fallen leaves and blossoms from the water surface.

Mom asks me whether I prefer Pepsi to Coke. I really can't decide. I like both, provided cold and with a big slice of lemon in the glass. Right after I come home from school, it is very refreshing. By and by, it becomes my signal for time off.

It is the time when smoking is permitted in every environment and the term "passive smoker" is not around yet and the dangers of it are unknown. In my host family, nobody smokes. I also have never noticed any consumption of alcohol there. Kim mentions several times that we are not old enough to buy alcoholic beverages at the supermarket. Neither can we order then in a restaurant or a bar. She makes it sound like socially unacceptable to drink at all. There were, though, as she concedes, some cheeky boys who bring beer to beach parties. One can of beer would be enough to get three people drunk. And as we all knew, to swim or surf in the Pacific Ocean while drunken was life-threatening.

Since the subject has come up, I repeat my wish to go to the beach on the weekend. Could we? I would love that.

"One to two hours 'drive, depending on the traffic and on the beach. But the season is only going to last for another month or so."

What? With it being so warm almost all year round? It is usually near 25° Celsius, which corresponds to 77 degrees Fahrenheit.

The common term is: "The temperature is in the high Seventies."

Often, people would say: "Sure glad we're not in Arizona. There in summer for weeks it gets up to 105 degrees. No chance without air conditioning."

I ask Kim if it ever got cold or did it ever rain?

"Only up North."

This is to mean the region around San Francisco, where, incidentally, all the water for South California comes from.

It doesn't seem to be scarce, since every family water their lawns, fill their swimming pools and wash their cars in the driveways.

There are car-wash facilities around everywhere, too. You don't even have to get out of the car in order to have it cleaned thoroughly. Once you mount the band, brushes come down, splashing the car from all sides with detergent and water and cleaning it. During the whole procedure, you only get out of the car once, when they come with huge vacuum cleaners to throughly vacuum in the inside. By the way, most cars have floor carpeting as well.

The workers there are all part-time, mostly high school or college students. It is not disgraceful at all, even for the children of rich families, to earn your pocket money in such a job.

After a few weeks, when Kim and I are quite familiar with each other, I decide to somehow find out more about her family. I have been wondering why Kim and Steph don't look alike at all. Kim is very slim; she has short brownish curls and brown eyes. Steph has got blue eyes, an extremely white skin and she wears her white-blonde hair shoulder length. Mom is a short, sturdy woman with greying hair. Dad is tall and almost bald.

Shortly afterwards, when Kim and I are sitting on our beds in the girls' room, doing homework, Kim suddenly gives me this penetrating look and says:

"I've got to tell you something. You know, we are adopted."

That is what I had thought. It is, by the way, perfectly all right with me. A childless couple giving a home to orphaned children. Mom and Dad must have somehow found each other when they were not so young any more, decided to stay together and adopt a little girl at the same time. The authorities took not long to notify them of a young woman in a precarious situation expecting a baby she would not be able to look after.

"You know, apparently my physical mother hesitated a lot before she agreed to give me away."

Images are rising in my head. A very young woman, unmarried, without any job qualification. She thinks:

"It will be the best solution for the child".

Right before birth, she is properly instructed. She may not see the baby. ("If you see it, you become attached.") When she hears it cry, she is not to react. Immediately, they will take her to another room.

They will tell her, though, whether it is a boy or a girl and if it is healthy or disabled.

Her breast would be fastened tightly right away. Then for a week or so, she would have to go about with a big towel tied around her body. The baby would be fed on a formula, which was healthier than mother's milk, anyway.

Six weeks later, the child would be handed over to his adoptive family. She could change her mind and claim him for herself during that time span only. Afterwards, there would be no way back.

A glance at Kimie tells me what I have come to know: a friendly, smart and pretty teenage girl she is. This might confirm the belief that the environment is dominant for the shaping of personality. Mom and Dad both seem to be happy. Kimie has obviously been brought up to act politely, work hard, study diligently while maintaining a critical approach.

When Kim was twelve years old, her parents decided to venture another adoption. But Steph soon proved to be difficult to integrate, crying very often and "needing lots of attention". Like an experienced psychologist, Kim explains to me the supposed reasons behind that behavior. I am truly impressed.

Presently, Kim goes on to tell me about the rest of her adoptive family. Mom has a sister who is married for the second time and has two biological children: a son already of age and a daughter, Manny, who is nineteen.

One day at the end of September, when Kim and I return home from school, all hell has broken loose. Mom's sister has committed suicide and Manny is all alone now.

This means, Manny is sitting, together with many others, in our living room and crying loudly. Mom, too, is yelling and crying on the top of her voice. The telephone and the doorbell keep on ringing alternately, it seems to us. Dad is nowhere to be seen. Kim is the only one keeping a cool head.

"For a while, we are going to have another sister. My cousin Manny is going to stay with us. She can sleep in my bed, it's big enough."

I start to get angry at this strange woman who just took her own life without the least consideration for her daughter.

Mom turns to me:

"Do you want to tell me how she did it? She pulled a dry cleaner's plastic bag over her head and put her head into the gas stove. The gas kept on streaming until they found her. Only good thing that the house didn't go up in flames."

When the meaning of her words hits home, I remain in a state of shock for some time.

Manny's whimpering goes on all night, although Kim had given her a "tranquilizer".

The next morning, our first news is about grandma, who had not survived the night.

Chapter 8

Satellite Telephones

The date is December 9th, 1965. 11 a.m. The ranks of the gym at Azusa High School are crowded with students and teachers. They are all eager to witness the event about to take place in front of their - ears.

Down on the parquetted floor, a huge screen has been put up. On a high table beside it, a telephone has been placed for everyone to see and in the middle of the two, there is me. I am not alone, a PR-man from General Telephone stands at an arm's length beside me and is talking nonstop into a microphone which he places under my nose whenever appropriate.

My answers come readily and quite excitedly. Yes, I am from Germany, from the South-West of it, near Heidelberg and the Black Forest. By this time, experience has taught me that these are the signal words at the mention of which eyes will light up.

Yes, I have written to my family and informed them of the oncoming call. I am allowed to talk as long as I want to! No, my family has no telephone. But the Holzbrecher family, with their daughter Monika being my classmate and best pal, for this special event has kindly agreed to invite to their home all people I would like to say a word to,

All people really means: many. Not only my family is on my list, but also friends and acquaintances. In a letter from the pastor of our parish, the Honorable Reverend Heffter, which I was to receive a week later, he writes what it was all about:

"To you, who have triggered a small trail of migration..."

The telephone man is meanwhile instructing the audience as to the function of a satellite transmitting conversation in a slide show. He solemnly announces the start of the age of wireless telephoning. He promises a faultless clarity regarding the transmission.

"You will understand every single word as clearly as if the speakers were in the very same room with us."

With tension mounting, he now asks me to introduce all my conversation partners. And of course, it would make sense to summarize at the end of every conversation what was said.

They answer the phone at the first dial tone.

My mother is piping:

"Iratshka, is that you?" (Iratshka of all names).

"Mama, I am calling you from America", I hear myself stammering, which is a completely redundant remark, mind you.

By and by, I am getting over my self-consciousness. I start talking happily and must have been grinning like a Cheshire cat, if one is to judge by the pictures which appeared in the local and school newspapers the next day.

With every new speaker, I turn towards the audience informing them who it is. As soon as we part, I translate the gist of our conversation. This way, half an hour is over before I even notice it.

My audience is fully concentrating and at the end, they ask a lot of questions.

No, I don't feel homesick.

Yes, it was very nice and I enjoyed it.

Oh yes, I like it here in California and I can easily imagine to live here (cheers).

At the end, our principal won't refrain from joining me on the floor. He seems pleased that everything went smoothly and thanks all participants for their cooperation.

"You were a great audience and I love you all! God bless you!" is the standard form of closing an address and I almost don't find it exaggerated any more.

Chapter 9

All the tricks a young dog can learn

The Californian (or American, for that matter) school system puts nearly all students into one type of school, but this doesn 't mean they all have the same classes. There surely is differentiation made according to knowledge, ability and talent/gift. Arguments for the slower learners being put at a disadvantage are unknown. Every student gets her due attention according to her aptitude.

I, for example was taken out of the math course "Calculus" after only one week of school. I just couldn't follow properly; it was as simple as that.

Instead, I was talked into taking "Home and Family" instead and now I have to do a paper about my own wedding. It is almost unanimously assumed that girls will get married very soon after their graduation from high school. I find this silly; I must admit.

Anyway, Kim and I set out to buy an illustrated periodical ("Bride's Magazine") from which I am to cut out the type of wedding dress I favor.

As if this wasn't bad enough, consequently I am to describe the type of man I would like to get married to. And all of this ado happens just because I am too dumb for calculus.

When I have slept over it and finally accept my fate, I choose Charlton Heston, because I had liked him in the movie "Quo vadis". Not that I had a crush on him or anything coming close to it, it might as well have been Robert Taylor or, for that matter, O.W. Fischer. Thinking about it, I chose an American film star, because Mrs. Kaymen in all probability wouldn 't have known whom I meant.

Does she know that there wouldn't have been any Hollywood without German actors and directors?

"You mean, Fritz Lang was German? How interesting."

Whom they commonly associate with German actors is "Marlin Dittrich" or "Hildgarde Neff".

In some circles in Europe, it is state of the art to mock about American public schools and their asserted "primitive level of education". I cannot support this view after everything I have observed and seen there. Not only school activities that last way into the afternoon, help to further, promote and encourage individual aptitude.

Let us now have a closer look at American teachers and their load of work which seems unbearable at first. Every morning, they teach, every afternoon, they guide special activities from homework monitoring to choir practice, from football coaching to drama rehearsing. In the evenings and at weekends, there are conferences, meetings with colleagues as well as with parents. Please note we have not yet talked about preparing lessons and correcting papers, neither about mandatory presence at school talent shows and games. For European ears, this sounds almost like slavery, for American teachers there is little problem involved.

In order to finally get down to it: Is there something wrong with European teachers? From decades of experience, I must put the blame on testing and examining systems.

Testing by multiple choice questions is much faster and doesn't produce different results from essay type exams, as many research papers have proved.

Am I implying that teachers in Europe should produce students who answer automatically and almost mechanically, even at ransom? Just mark the right letter and, in the end, not learn how to articulate or write any sentence correctly? That is by no means what will be the outcome. Of course, American students, too, have to be able to write a composition, there are even special courses for it, not only English, which is required throughout their schooling career. Debating also plays and important role in afternoon activities. The art of rhetoric is taught and tested in countless competitions, mostly inter-school ones.

Moreover, when a student promises to possess genuine talent, there is special support available in Europe as well as in the States. On the other hand, students needing exceedingly careful attention will be placed in the corresponding institutions, as of today, fortunately there is still money allocated to their needs as well.

Coming back to your average student, how does she know which courses are suitable for her? The American advisor system is ideally suited to bring out the best in every individual student. Your advisor does not necessarily need to be a teacher, he can be loosely connected to the job, an educator working part time or even any teaching assistant. Since teachers are not counted among the better paid working force, advisors are neither. In some regions, for instance, many parents volunteer as advisors, taking special preparatory courses and obtaining the appropriate certificates. Motivated and serious advisors are often even ready to help correcting tests.

Only as late as the beginning of the 21st century, German schools have started to hire advisors. But if I student is referred to them, you can be sure it is because she is a troublemaker of some kind. In general, the class teacher is at the same time the special advisor of every student in his class. When done diligently, this turns out to be much too time-consuming.

Another big problem that takes up time beyond reason is our high school certificate. I am by no means implying that everything is better in the States, but the procedures needed to end your secondary school career certainly are. There are no lengthy extra central exams towards the end of the final school year. There are, in addition to regular testing, final examinations at the end of every school year.

Considering that every educational institution has a limited number of places available, how do universities and vocational colleges decide whom they admit?

They decide according to grades, grade average, letters of recommendation and sometimes, aptitude tests. There is a general test called SAT (Scholastic Aptitude Test) which is not mandatory, though. And then (in my time in California) there was the College Entrance Examination Board which administered tests at special centers all over the country and in befriended countries as well. When I decided in 1967, after my concluded high school career in Germany, that I wanted to continue my studies at the

American Robert College in Istanbul, I was examined at Heidelberg, where there was a US base with a school for their military personnel attached to it.

College education, though, contrary to primary and secondary one, is not for free. In addition, expenses for living on campus and for books and diverse things are left up to the student or her parents. University education is therefore much cheaper in Europe.

On the other hand, in the USA, there are countless scholarships for poor and eager students. State scholarships, private institutions and churches grant conditional and unconditional funding.

To come to the core of it, finishing high school and going on to university has a somewhat more prestigious meaning in Europe, where blue collar workers and white-collar workers are still definitely of different status. In America, the aim is to send all students to school for 12 years, regardless of their capacity. This is meant to be the same type of school for almost everyone, which, in turn, differentiates the courses offered, in proportion to age, prerequisites and talent. Certainly, there are mandatory courses for every age level as well. When there are enough students available, these courses run parallel to each other, primarily looking at previously obtained grades.

There are courses in the afternoon with a definite vocational touch, like for technically interested students. But there is no leaving school after eight years, let's say, and starting work while still attending a vocational school once a week. What we call the "dual school system" is practically unknown. Even in college, really sought-after, sophisticated candidates are following an undergraduate university schedule until, usually after two, but for subjects like medicine after four years, they are ready to concentrate on their particular subjects. Most students take up a job at some time during their university careers.

For all students to hold on, even for the disabled and no-interest ones, there are countless motivators built in. The graduation ceremony is one of them. When the diplomas are handed over, everybody together with family and friends, meets in the big stadium of the town. The graduates are all wearing the same cap and gowns and rituals which are the intrinsic part of many a student's dreams and aims.

The last year of high school is rather demanding. Students are not only busy studying, but also applying to different colleges and universities for their further education. In order to make it look as attractive as possible, there are parties, festivities and Senior privileges. There is the school ring in different sizes for boys and girls, the Senior key, to be worn around your neck, that is events and objects to make the Senior status look special and desirable. To be good in sports is the most prestigious excellence. The assumption that every person is able to execute at least one type of sport, is never questioned. Whatever sport you can think of, you will be helped to practice it. Again, there are signs and symbols to show your engagement, like varsity (the selected best performers of their kind) lettermen jackets and other unmistakable gear.

If you are liable and leaning towards arts or social activities, teachers and advisors will show you possibilities to realize your creative potential.

But, alas, if you don't keep going till the end, you are branded as a "drop-out" and will have a hard time to find any kind of job.

Mentioning jobs: Besides school and extra-curricular activities, a greater part of the Seniors has odd jobs from time to time or even on a regular basis. When wondering, how many hours of sleep they do get, most of them will state (tongue in cheek) that there will be time for peace and quiet, once they are in the coffin.

Consequently, one of my school pals one day asks me if I wouldn't like to do odd jobs from time to time, as well. She works as a party hostess in mansions of Hollywood stars and starts counting to me all the people's home she knew and whom all she had met.

So, around Christmas, Mae West is throwing a stand-up party for a large number of guests and Jane and I are among the hostesses. Of course, I am very curious to see the movie stars in person. I hadn't ever heard of Mae West, though. In the Forties, she was supposed to have been one of the swinging vamps in Hollywood, a real man-eater, so to speak. Her home is half way up the nob hill and from the outside it looks like most of the neighboring estates, hidden behind walls and trees. It turns out to be fancy Bauhaus-style with an oriental touch in the interior.

"I am going to introduce you to Miss West. Just say 'How do you do?' Nothing else. She likes to be formal. You know, she is very old."

When Jane has presented me to the hostess, she remarks loftily:

"Wonderful! How good her English is!"

I am busy following the instructions my experienced fellow student keeps on giving me I am trying to be charming, nice; I smile, greet the new arrivals and show them where they will find everything.

By and by, the room is filling, the cocktails are getting spilled and the floor is starting to get slippery. Suddenly, I overhear Miss West say:

"Men! Talk to men about the weather! The only weather they care about is whether you will or whether you won't."

At midnight Jane and I have to leave. We get 30 $ each, just a little over what we spent for professional hairdos and make-up. Tipping, by the way, is very high in the US; you are expected to give at least 15% of your bill.

The valet parking attendant get us our car without any comment, let alone niceties. We are bluntly made aware of the fact that we don't belong to the generously tipping in-crowd.

Soon afterwards we get another offer for a party in Bel Air. The host is Jack Benny, his star guest is Sally Rand. This time, I am wearing a silver pink brocade dress I borrowed and long white gloves to go with it. Again, I find that people are especially polite towards me because I am a foreigner, a visitor from Europe. My job is to show the arriving guests the memory book and smilingly hand them a ballpoint pen, saying in a sweet voice:

"Would you please sign your name here, sir/madam?"

In the hostesses dressing room, some of the varied finger food appetizers are set out for us to try, too. In the reception hall, butlers in full gear including white gloves are skillfully balancing their trays from group to group. As far as drinks go, we are only allowed water, not only because we are supposed to stay sober, but also because we are under age.

The flash person of the evening is an aging burlesque dancer named Sally Rand. She is wearing a tightly fitting low-cut glamour outfit. She addresses me gracefully and even drops a little party-talk in my direction. When she is handed the microphone and starts telling jokes, I am not the only one who is absolutely shocked.

The legendary diva must have noticed my mimics, since after the thunder of applause has ceased, she comes up right to me and continues talking as before: like a real lady. Is she acting the lady or the vamp? Whatever, the sudden transformation is amazing.

After this evening, I decide not to do this type of job again. I need to organize my free time and use it well. If I want to earn a little pocket money, I should opt for babysitting, I reckon. So many girls who work as a party hostess do aspire a career as a movie star. Just to meet a few second-rate Hollywood actors, like Jane admits loving to do, I don't find so thrilling. I have never wanted to become an actress. Although Mae West and Sally Rand are still known and around at that time, the real stars are coming to top colleagues or business people only, I am informed. And they sometimes even get paid if they show up. Invitations are sent to money, fame, beauty and originality – in this exact order.

In May 1966, when all my classmates are receiving their admissions to college, Jane is very happy to announce that she has got a scholarship for one of the most prestigious acting departments of a state university. Once again, she recites to us the passages from Lorca's "The House of Bernarda Alba" which she had selected for her hearing. The jury had given her an A.

I am impressed. She is really good, completely free of stage fever and very stage present. This, she mostly owes to the drama club at school, of which she has been a diligent and eager member, rehearsing almost every afternoon, coached by a retired English teacher and former hobby actress.

Chapter 10

Midterm Grades

Local state schools are frequented by almost everyone. Private schools are something very exclusive. The most prestigious ones are military academies. Europeans in general are not aware of how disciplined and strictly regulated the institutions of educational character really are in the States, and not only those.

From an early age on, Americans are expected to be objective in their self-evaluation, always striving to improve their performance. At first, I am puzzled with this phenomenon, having been taught by general agreement not to excel or show blatant ambition. It almost had a vulgar touch to compete with classmates for the best results. In sports, it was different, though. Soon I come to understand the philosophy underlying this constant thriving for competition and excellence: Everything is considered a sport and the sportsman, whatever sport he may be talented for or choosing to perform, finds fulfillment in perfection.

My grades at Azusa High School are good enough, only in Government I get a C. I am kind of hurt, because Mr. Clark, my teacher, always commends and encourages me.

In Beginning Spanish, I get an A+ and am being transferred right away to the next higher Spanish course. The teacher, Dr. Nelida Constenla, a young lady from Argentina, is the same. She is an example for good manners and many of us, consciously or unconsciously, strive to imitate her. Polite, patient and friendly, she retains control over young troublemakers, mostly of Latin American origin, who make up the greater part of her class.

Her mission is evident: She striving to transfer her admiration for her beautiful language. It is the time when the military Foreign Language Institute in Monterey sets out to remodel language teaching: the secret is supposed to be oral replacement and repetition exercises ("pattern practice").

This kind of exercises, especially when taking place in the so-called Language Lab in separate boxes and with head phones on and microphones sticking out in front, are bound to create boredom. A student without any real motivation and self-discipline will let her thoughts wander after a short time.

So, Mrs. Constenla makes use of a combination of traditional classroom teaching and excursions to the Lab. In the classroom, students are allowed to raise their hands and ask whatever questions they may have. In general, teachers are careful not to just cut them off.

Jose, the impudent trouble-maker type, loves to interrupt Mrs. Constenla's lectures by doing everything to get her attention.

"Mrs. Constenla, why are the Argentinians so hostile against America?"

"You know, Gomez, nobody wants their neighbors to interfere with their private affairs, right? Like when your neighbor told you what to plant in your backyard or when Rodriguez criticized your clothes, would you like that?"

The first time she uses this technique, I am surprised, having expected a completely different type of reply like reprimanding or a simple retort to keep to the issue. Maybe, under the influence of our daily morning ceremonies, I would also have opted for a diplomatic answer or maybe a soothing or even an evasive one.

I remember this short episode so well, because it was almost like a sudden flash of recognition for me: this emigrant lady loves and defends her country of origin, the way many Americans love their country unconditionally.

My French teacher, on the other side, is a fully-fledged American with the obligatory accent included. Whenever an American native speaker pronounces a French word, he invariably cultivates the same accent, I soon discover. Later on, taking linguistic courses at university level, I come to understand that native speakers of English are inclined to pronounce almost all vowels as diphthongs. But at this time in high school, I am getting irritated at my teacher 's saying "vo-u" instead of "vu". Her daily repeating of Bo-u-shurr, komo-untalleyvo-u keeps provoking my inner objection. In French, I get an A-.

My absolute favorite subject, though, is Lit & Comp with Mr. Mullen. He is well-read, motivated and easy-going. We love him and hang on his every word. Since then, I have ever so often remembered his famous mantra:

"Read it now and wake up! If you don't wake up now, you wouldn't wake up if the Azusa Marching Band passed by your window."

Mr. Mullen is a friend and connoisseur of classical Russian literature. He manages to whet our appetite by introducing first short pieces of universal themes like "The Captain's Daughter" by Pushkin, from there going on to Gogol's "Dead Souls" until he finally presents us with Tolstoy. We are surprised and delighted by the shrewd humor and fine irony of Gogol. We get involved and ask our teacher about details, not being surprised at his announcement that Gogol had to flee to Italy and stay a few years until his obvious impudence was forgotten and he was no longer considered dangerous for the political authorities. In those days, when the pen could still be mightier than the sword.

And who would have thought that Pushkin left a legacy of over a hundred ladies' names and addresses when he unfortunately died at an early age, during a duel for a lady's honor.

Remembering seeing the opera "Eugen Onegin" a year before in Munich with my mother who had talked me into accompanying her, I felt empathy for the greatest classical writer of Russia. The opera is about a woman who resists giving in to her first love, ten years after she had shyly wooed him and been rejected. Surely Pushkin must have longed for an angel of moral integrity, never having met one. Or maybe there had been a woman who was strong enough to refuse him and he had taken her as a model for his heroine Tatiana.

Cullen often assigned us to read 100 pages or more till the next class meeting. It was sure a time-consuming lot, but if you love literature, it doesn't feel like a burden. You even read more than that, homework or not. Yet there were times when all assignments were almost impossible to accomplish, meaning: extensive reading for enjoyment was out. So, we went to the library and searched the index drawers for summaries and literary criticism which actually turned out to be as time consuming as reading. But it opened new perspectives for us and we discussed different approaches and learned to defend our own point of view. Group work was an established part of Lit&Comp, though the time allowed was never enough.

Mr. Kaymen is one of the AFS volunteers looking after foreign exchange students. On a Saturday, he takes me to Beverly Hills in his new Cadillac to show me where the real Hollywood stars live. It is hard to even get a glimpse at the houses from the outside, almost all mansions are hidden behind walls and hedges and barely visible from the street. He points them out to me, dropping famous names. The road is leading uphill in serpentines. It is a quiet, well-groomed neighborhood radiating wealth.

Willy Kaymen knows that behind every wall there is a security system including cameras, safety precaution devices and personnel.

"I have never heard of such a thing in Germany", I hear myself saying, unable to hide how much I am impressed by all these.

"Germany is about 30 years behind the US ", Kaymen lectures to me. "In technology, in business as well as in medicine. Take your shoes. Why are you still wearing leather shoes, if new materials have been created which combine all good qualities of leather with much more convenient ones added by artificial ingredients? The ultimate shoes don't need any leather, they are completely man-made."

Something is bothering me. My provincial upbringing combined with a sudden feeling of attachment to the land where I was brought up cause me to rebel.

"I like leather shoes. They are the real thing. They have class."

Kaymen is grinning: "You little snob."

In Bel Air we treat ourselves to a generous scoop of ice-cream and end the day by dropping into his home. His wife is just changing the baby's diapers and the look on her face is as sinister and rejecting as can be.

"What's wrong, honey?" Kaymen asks her, suddenly abashed.

She almost bursts with anger and yells at him:

"Wrong? What's wrong? I have been left here all by myself on a lovely Saturday afternoon, knowing my husband is driving around with an attractive young lady!"

It takes me a few seconds to understand what is going on and I find her way out. Never ever would I have dreamed of considering my outing with the AFS man a date.

Kaymen hisses something into her ear and quickly adds, louder now:

"Well, I'll be back in a second. Let me take the student back to her foster family first."

Thinking hard whether I should say something, too, I manage to remark embarrassedly:

"Bye, Mrs. Kaymen. Sorry we took so long. What a cute baby."

When I tell Kim what happened, she waves it off, announcing at the same time an exciting trip to San Diego, which is planned for the next weekend. Immediately, my thoughts jump to the Saturday ahead and I start imagining how things would look there, so close to Mexico!

Chapter 11

War in Paradise

That is what most Germans long for and dream of when they think of holiday incarnate: Sun on end, royal blue sky, some whitewashed houses colonial style, southern vegetation and in the middle of all of it tanned bathers sporting relaxed dress.

My host family is taking me on an outing to San Diego, a town in south-western California, bordering on Mexico. We are staying at a middle-class motel – according to American standards. The rooms are spacious with huge spring beds, adjacent bathrooms with little wrapped-up soaps, TV, water boiler, menu lists and a telephone for free local calls, I am allowed to ring up the local AFSer, a boy from the Black Forest named Pit.

He is radiating good mood and happiness, so glad to be able to babble on in our common vernacular, Swabian. I come to realize how much I had missed my local dialect. Pit says he will drop by to see me. Mom doesn't allow it.

What the heck. Then we'll just talk on the phone. Pit is showing off to me:

"From my window I can even see Mexico. And the big harbor of San Diego, if you know what I mean. The hills, the condos, the streets and the docks, the people who have come to pick up the arriving passengers, waiting behind barriers. Most ships bring returning veterans. Many are wounded and being carried on stretchers. The only thing I cannot see from here is the coffins. They are being unloaded in a different place."

I am starting to feel bad. Blurred memories from stories my parents have told me about the war are returning all of a sudden.

"What if the Vietnamese come and bomb San Diego harbor?"

Pit just cannot stop laughing aloud.

"Imagine the geography and history lessons you must have had back in Heilbronn!"

I there and then decide to ask Mr. Clark about this war in detail. For several times I have talked to Americans being proud of their soldiers and of their sons who died in combat.

Later Clark tells me that there are also voices who speak of the senselessness of that war and are trying to convince the government to stop it. But as history will show, this really meaningless killing was to be continued on both sides for years to come.

"Ireyney, we are going to the pool. If and when you decide to join us, here is the key. Don't forget to look the door, when you are finished talking."

In the afternoon we are invited to a Mexican family in an almost exclusively Latin-American neighborhood. Inside the house, I notice a different arrangement from the standard Californian one. There is less furniture, mostly made of wickerwork, and lots of decoration, the color gold being dominant. Chairs and stools are made from carved wood or held together with ropes. In a corner of the living room there is a sort of shrine or altar with a crucifix on the wall and on an extended shelf below it, a statue of the Virgin as well as other little deco figurines and photos in golden frames. In the bedrooms, there are smaller counterparts of it.

The women of the house are wearing colorful dresses with crocheted lace on the seams and hems. They have pretty faces and thick, long black hair. But their figures are not the equivalent of the skinny American ideal. They speak "Spanglish", a creole language consisting of Central American Spanish and US English vocab.

"Your language is your home" is a saying that I have often since come to reaffirm.

Kim never tires to explain and brief and lecture. The neighborhood we are visiting is not considered poor at all.

"Most Mexicans live in poverty. Their work ethics are different from ours and besides, they have large families to feed."

I start to feel an omnipresent love for music, for rhythm, creating a good mood and relaxed atmosphere. People make musical instruments from pumpkins, from dried grasses and twigs. Percussion and wood winds have been the classics ever since the beginning of human culture. Singing and humming is in the air, rhythmic dance steps follow.

People living in San Diego need no heating and no winter clothes. The good news is that it never gets unbearably hot either, because more often than not, a cool breeze comes in from the ocean.

Unless, like it happens once in a while, the winds blow directly from the Mexican subcontinent, whirling hot air into the valleys of California and keeping the exhaust gases down in the basins of the towns. Then you surely will be out of breath.

One day, walking home from school, I am caught by surprise - of seeing nothing. Everything is submerged in a yellow-whitish haze. Is it fog? Then why does it cut off my breath? I start breathing more and more heavily and gulping for air until every breath hurts.

"All wrong!" Steph crows triumphantly. "You are supposed not to breathe, but instead hold a Kleenex over your mouth and nose!"

My chest hurts and even the comparatively clear air inside the house does not bring immediate relief.

"Well, sorry, I should have told you about a Santa Ana", Kim admits ruefully.

"But this one came really fast, almost as a surprise. – Gosh, your eyes are all red, why don't you take a shower and I'll get us some ice cream."

Santana is the name of this notorious weather condition, which causes many people to make for the mountains as fast as they can. The next morning, the spook is over, but for days I keep on having pains when breathing.

Chapter 12

California is liberal

On June 3rd, 2019, the author Anthony Francis DiPrima decided to publish on Facebook the impressions Col. Larry Carrigan had retained from a visit of "Peace Activist" Jane Fonda showing up in the prison camp of the Vietcong.

"From 1963-65, Col. Larry Carrigan was in the 47FW/DO (F-4E's). He spent 6 years in the "Hanoi Hilton". . . The first three of which his family only knew he was "missing in action." His wife lived on faith that he was still alive. His group, too, got the cleaned-up, fed and clothed routine in preparation for a "peace delegation" visit.

They, however, had time and devised a plan to get word to the world that they were alive and still survived. Each man secreted a tiny piece of paper, with his Social Security Number on it, in the palm of his hand. When paraded before Ms. Fonda and a cameraman, she walked the line, shaking each man's hand and asking little encouraging snippets like: "Aren't you sorry you bombed babies?" and "Are you grateful for the humane treatment from your benevolent captors?" Believing this HAD to be an act, they each palmed her their sliver of paper.

She took them all without missing a beat. . . At the end of the line and once the camera stopped rolling, to the shocked disbelief of the POWs, she turned to the officer in charge and handed him all the little pieces of paper...

Three men died from the subsequent beatings. Colonel Carrigan was almost number four but he survived, which is the only reason we know of her actions that day.

I was a civilian economic development adviser in Vietnam, and was captured by the North Vietnamese communists in South Vietnam in 1968, and held prisoner for over 5 years.

I spent 27 months in solitary confinement; one year in a cage in Cambodia; and one year in a 'black box' in Hanoi. My North Vietnamese captors deliberately poisoned and murdered a female missionary, a nurse in a leprosarium in Banme Thuot, South Vietnam, whom I buried in the jungle near the Cambodian border. At one time, I weighed only about 90 lbs. (My normal weight is 170 lbs.)

We were Jane Fonda's "war criminals."

When Jane Fonda was in Hanoi, I was asked by the camp communist political officer if I would be willing to meet with her. I said yes, for I wanted to tell her about the real treatment we POWs received. . . and how different it was from the treatment purported by the North Vietnamese, and parroted by her as "humane and lenient."

Because of this, I spent three days on a rocky floor on my knees, with my arms outstretched with a large steel weight placed on my hands, and beaten with a bamboo cane.

I had the opportunity to meet with Jane Fonda soon after I was released. I asked her if she would be willing to debate me on TV. She never did answer me."

But now we are in the year 1966 and for American teens the world is still in good order. There were the good ones and on the other side, the bad ones. And besides, there also were the leftists, secretly admired for their daring and courage and rebel spirit. Young people tend to have a weakness for rebels. The film "Rebel without a Cause "(1959) with James Dean and also the growing popularity of Elvis Presley might serve as typical examples for the era to come and to turn upside down all traditional values.

At that time, though, Jane Fonda had not yet displayed any interest in politics nor could she be labelled an ambiguous peace activist. She was then Barbarella from the movie with the same name, discovered recently by the French film director Roger Vadim, who had already made popular Brigitte Bardot.

The remarkable intro to that science fiction drama was filmed and cut in a way to show Fonda hovering through space in perfect nakedness, passing all censorship criteria. Never once was there a glimpse of either her nipples or her private parts. That would have been forbidden.

To sum it up, the generation of the so-called 68ers in California were mostly conformists, some were sceptics, a few though, were active war opponents and thus brandmarked as traitors. Some of my classmates got their draft cards even before graduation. I know boys who burned them and turned out to be scorned as cowards.

But they were not discriminated against by everybody alike. The longer the Vietnam war lasted, the more anti-war voices were heard. While some parents still boasted in public that "they had two sons in Vietnam", more and more details of that senseless massacre came to light.

If you asked me, why no earlier and not more protesters came out among young Americans, I would attribute it to their emotional allegiance to the flag, which on the one hand gave them a feeling of togetherness and belonging but on the other hand also made it more difficult to reflect critically.

Walt Whitman against Bob Dylan, maybe that was it. Besides, at that time there was practically no American who didn't want to be American, so to speak.

When I was a 17-year-old teenager, I was not able to sort out all these impressions I had. I was an AFSer, a little ambassador of my own country, lecturing in front of NGOs and other groups. The local AFS committee in Heilbronn had forewarned me to take along slides which could illustrate my talks. So, I was armed with pictures obtained from Heilbronn County Media and some from Berlin as well. They came in useful when giving speeches to Lions, Rotarian, Soroptimists and others.

In this way, I also met my first Jewish family. I got invited to their Chanukah celebration and I was very much impressed. My positive attitude towards Jewish college friends and their families in Istanbul, Turkey, might also have originated on this first visit. The tender stronghold of the family as a whole, I observed, was the same on either side of the Atlantic.

At that time, I found out that Jews in California preferred to stay among their own kind. Although contact with members of other denominations was common and quite relaxed, marriages between Jewish women and e.g., Christian men were considered a taboo.

I was also invited to homes of fellow students, among them the family of a bright, eloquent and sanguine girl by the name of Ann. This encounter was to determine the rest of my stay in the U.S. I liked being with her family so well that it didn't take much to persuade me to leave my host home and move in with them. My mom was always busy forbidding me this and that. Kim was a great girl and sister for that matter, but she was always busy with something important and quite serious in character. Dad I hardly saw and as to Steph, I have already referred to her as being the snotty little sister, often left out and trying to live up to the two big rivals.

After a dramatic attempt at reconciliation which ended in tears, Mrs. Roberts, the local AFS representative, soon gave way to my request, noticing well the obvious relief the change would bring to me.

Consequently, I moved in with the family V. Dad was a teacher, Mom was a perfect housekeeper, also very much involved in the social life of the community. Ann had a sister, one year her junior, Kerry, and a little brother, Mike, who was about Steph's age.

It was easily predictable that Kim would be very hurt. I felt guilty towards her, though unable to regret my decision. In the long run, I learned that Kim had become a competent teacher, acting at the same time as a consultant for highly gifted children and ended up in the neighbor state of Colorado, as a board member of a scholarship foundation.

In my new family, everybody seemed to be not only nice, but also very good-looking. The two girls might as well have been counted as explicitly beautiful. They both had full, chestnut-color hair of their mother's and the expressive blue eyes of their father.

We are still in the year 1966 and California is considered liberal, officially not discriminating anyone, treating the few black inhabitants (today this expression is considered politically incorrect) with casual politeness. The Afro-American social studies teacher at Azusa High School, Mr. James Clark, is very popular and, in a way, the pride of the teaching staff.

Una Morris, an exchange student from Jamaika, is very modest, unobtrusive and at the same time a tough first-class athlete. She was later to make it to a participation a the Olympic Games, gradually becoming a medical doctor in radiology going back and forth between hospital duty and her own office.

The few Afro-Americans living in California are never a cause for complaint, moreover, well-behaved "whites" do sport an ostentatious, friendly way with them. Nevertheless, they certainly are aware of their not quite belonging.

According to today's criteria of political correctness, my observations of the 1960ties are outmoded, unimportant and even in danger of being misunderstood for transmitting "racist potential". Yet, every society and every era has got their own unwritten laws which can be felt but never completely defined.

Chapter 13

Useful for life

I'm learning how to type. I have borrowed from the library a booklet called " Teach yourself Typing ". It was one of the best decisions I've ever made regarding my professional life. Working through two pages every day, that's what I have set out to do.

The typewriters of the time were not easy to use, but on the other hand, it was easier to notice if you hit the wrong key because the keys were not as flat as they are today on the computer keyboard and even more so on the smartphone.

However, on every side of the manual you are reminded to write blindly and to resist the temptation to look at your hands. It was annoying. Before the introduction of the ball-type typewriter, a letter could not simply be deleted by pressing the back key; for this purpose. There were individually wrapped little white erasing pads that were placed between the key and the fixed paper sheet.

Unfortunately, I gave up when I got through and had mastered all the letters. So even today, I am still looking at the keyboard for numbers and special characters. From then on, I could do my homework on the typewriter, very soon, I also typed my letters home.

Since I also had to take on chores in the household, I learned from Ann and Kerry how to do the dishes in a deep sink and, of course, the order in which they were washed. At first it bothered me that the dog's bowl was also thrown in together with the normal dishes, then I got used to it.

Ann, Kerry and I would switch tasks every three weeks: one of us laid the table, the other washed the dishes and the third one dried and stowed them in their proper places.

Ironing shirts and blouses quickly but properly was also a matter of practice: spraying starch on them, ironing first the collar from back to front, straightening the shoulders with your left hand while the right one is adjusting the iron. Then the back, and finally the front, with the buttons closed all the time, even when washing it and finally when putting it on and taking it off. The sleeves come at the end, starting with the cuffs. Then the shirt is pulled onto a hanger and placed on the bar in the closet. There is a lot of space there, because for a wardrobe, usually one wall of each bedroom is provided, at a length of around 70 centimeters, with a floor rail and two slide doors.

The climate in the coastal and lower regions of California being moderate throughout the year, most homes are of lightweight construction, made mainly from wood and plastic. There is no basement, no insulation. They have sliding windows and mosquito screens in front of them, the floors are dressed with simple laminate or just covered with wall-to-wall carpeting. Where wood has been used, it is usually coated with paint in a very light color. In the 1960s, heating device is only visible as air vents at the top of the walls. Outside the house, as well as in front and in the back, there is yard for playing, for growing vegetables and flowers, also for drying racks and waste bins.

California also proved to be a "school for life" for me in other ways. My new mom went with me to the local Citrus College, where there was a "Cosmetology" department, an institution comparable to European apprenticeship as a hairdresser and beautician. There she presented me as an exemplary case desperately needing a new hair style. So, I was an object for study in a class and the students gave detailed advice on how my hair should be cut and cared for in the future. The haircut I got cost nothing, and in due time I also learned how to put up my hair in curlers.

The curlers of the time were smooth and had to be held together with hair clips so they wouldn't fall off. Most women and girls slept all night with their hair rolled up, over which they fixed an elastic hair net. Lying on their side, they stretched one arm upwards so that it served as a support for the face and the rigid curlers would be less annoying.

But this ordeal was nothing compared to that of women who went to the hairdresser and wanted to wear their expensive hairdo for a day longer and therefore, lying on their backs, put a hard, bone-shaped pillow under their necks, not moving all night to avoid taking on a different position.

At that time, I also started to use the make-up utensils of my new foster sister and soon bought my own ones.

Back then, many of the schoolgirls wore dresses from the "Sears and Roebuck" mail order company, where I also ordered two items. My first shock was the real price, which in the whole U.S. is still not properly stated, neither in the shop, nor in the adds, nor in the catalogue. The value added tax is a matter between the government, and the purchaser. Thus, it doesn't appear on the price tag either. Of course, neither do the shipping costs.

Old mail order customers know from earlier times that the colors and even the cut of mail order ware were allowed to deviate from their illustrations in the catalogue. It was no different in America. In such a case, the package contents would be accompanied by the laconic message, stating that a 'similar' product was being delivered due to high demand. All of this was legal, including the fact that some customers had to wait for weeks to get their order. A lot has happened since then in terms of consumer protection. But later, because of the right to send everything back, goods were often first trimmed to appear as new, and today returned delivery is simply being destroyed. Because time is money, as Benjamin Franklin already stated in 1748.

The American (and also English) custom of sliding into bed like a letter being put into an envelope, is also something not easily accepted by people from Central Europe, for example. If you pulled out the sheets at night, you would have trouble making the bed the next day. On the other hand, it is quite okay if you just tuck the upper part of the blanket with the linen underneath under the spring-bed mattress on the right and left. When compared to our large ones, the rather narrow American pillows don't feel strange any more after a few nights.

All of this quickly comes natural to you. Getting used really works better the younger a person is and the less often she repeats the old procedure. No wonder that the Trojans of antiquity were said to have burned their ships when they fled to Sicily after their 10-years-war. Going back and forth is much more difficult than consistently following one line. I had to experience this later in life when I started my college years in Istanbul, from where I visited Germany quite frequently for twenty years' time.

In 1966 I surely would have quickly become a convinced American if I had not returned to Germany at the end of July, as agreed.

Together with Christmas and New Year's Eve celebrations, my birthday which falls into that season stands out vividly in my memory

In the morning, I wake up in painful surprise, when my host sister Kerry hits me on the arm 17 times, almost spanking me, accompanying every stroke with a "Happy Birthday", which she sang in her beautiful soprano voice. I am torn between crying out "Ouch, stop it" and listening to the voice of reason telling me to withstand every single stroke till 17 had been reached.

Meanwhile, ma little host brother Mike is trying out his new drum, a Christmas present from Santa Claus. From the kitchen, Mom's voice is heard languishing for a white Christmas in a heartbreaking manner. Daddy is watching the morning news on TV and Ann has put on her favorite record, singing along with the Beatles "Day tripper, Sunday driver, yeah".

The breakfast table has been laid out with special care; I notice. My place is sprinkled with presents, all wrapped up with care and sporting ribbons of many colors. I likewise show my thankfulness and admire every single one with due sounds and thanks. Now is the time to also open my birthday letters and to share my happiness with the whole family. Otherwise, nothing unusual happens until in the evening, when Ann casually suggests we drop by our classmate Brian.

Brian's mother opens the door calling out a heartful "Happy Birthday". She asks us into the living room which seems to be completely in the dark. But immediately we find ourselves surrounded by burning sparklers, a turning ball of light and the shine of candles. A shower of confetti and rising balloons serve to round up the scene.

Cries of "Surpriiiise!" are heard and the music begins to play at full volume, accompanying the voices of my classmates serenading me with "Happy Birthday". Since I had never before heard or seen anything like this, it takes me a second to close my mouth again. But I remember feeling overwhelmed by pure joy and happiness at that thrilling experience.

For the second time that day I am unwrapping gifts, mostly cosmetics and perfume, even perfumed clothes hangers, all wrapped in shiny material with little bags full of scent dangling from them. And there is a big powder case with loose white powder in it and a fancy powder puff on top. This is, I am told, applied to your body after showering, the best method to "stay cool" on a hot day.

As Brian starts to play music, we dance the "mashed potatoes" and the "soup spoon". Sounds quite harmless? Do them and feel your sore muscles ache the next day.

Around midnight, Peggy is arriving with a huge square cake with sugar icing and candles on top. She had lit the candles before coming in and there was something written on the cake 'Herrliche, gluckliche Geburtstag" I read aloud. Maybe I even cried a little. I don't quite remember.

"Ann, why didn't you warn me of what was to happen?", I later ask her, which was a completely redundant question, of course. Quick-witted Ann has a wonderful sense of humor and simply retorts:

"Because it was going to be a surprise!"

I now seem to have become what the Americans call "popular". One of my classmates has nominated me for Christmas Queen and it turns out I will be one of the princesses at the Christmas dance. Mom sews me a long dress of flock printed organdy, my host sister Ann gives me long, white fancy gloves to go with it.

That same dress I also wear to the New Year's Eve dance, where I am again caught by surprise when on the dance floor at midnight my date starts kissing me without warning.

I stare at him, puzzled, at the same time noticing all the couples around us engaged in long kisses. Now the loudspeakers are sounding with "Auld lang syne". Some of the people on the floor join in and I, too, start singing in, since I know the tune and words from my English lessons.

A feeling of grateful remembering mounts as I remember Herrn Mörke, my English teacher from Elly-Heuss-Knapp-Gymnasium, back home. In his lessons, he used to work a lot with songs, singing them to us all by himself, which was by no means considered normal at the time. We sang along and after the first time, nobody grinned bashfully any more.

We knew from hearsay that he had been rescued by propellor plane from the kettle of Stalingrad, heavily wounded. Since these words meant nothing and rang no bell at all, we could but repeat them with sternness, the way they had been told to us.

Despite his prosthetic leg, he walked upright. Being involuntarily and almost unconsciously awed by and his tall figure, his full white hair, his zealous efforts as a teacher along with his broad knowledge left a lasting impression on us. We were never as attentive as in his classes, feeling we owed it to him. Maybe that is the secret of a teacher's: be a good example, evoke respect and stimulate curiosity.

Mörke is at the core of why I am dancing, all dressed up, here in Southern California on New Year's Eve of 1965.

Well, not only him, but also other well-meaning teachers, among them (Miss) Dr. Ilse Odernheimer, who first got me interested in the English language and helped me develop and nourish it.

The end of the year is really full of events.

On January 1st, after the dance, I am supposed to "stay the night" with Maggie and her family. But when we arrive there around 2.30 a.m., Mrs. Roberts of AFS is already waiting for us. I have to change into my casual clothes quickly, because we are heading for Los Angeles to see the Rose Parade and we want to get a good look at all the floats and carts, bands and other groups taking part in it. It reminds me of our carnival parades where one float follows the other, all of them adorned and decorated all over. Moreover, right after the parade, the first football game of the year is going to be staged in the Rose Bowl, which is a gigantic stadium.

The Los Angeles Times states the number of spectators at around two million. Wherever the corso is planned to pass along, people have been assembling with sleeping bags and little tents since the early evening before. They all want to cheer when their schools or clubs' parade past them.

At five o'clock in the morning we are finally there, after having successfully parked the car and walked for an estimated mile.

Everything is regulated and arranged to avoid chaos and confusion before they could start. On both sides of the streets, portable tribunes have been erected. Alcohol is strictly forbidden and many policemen and volunteers are patrolling the rows. There is no rowdy making or other misbehavior. The people already there tell us freely how early they have come and how cold they have felt at times, in spite of their sleeping bags.

Southern California can be considered a warm country, but around New Year it is apt to get cold, even down to 10° centigrade. When you say it in Fahrenheit, it sounds much milder though ("in the Fifties").

When the music finally becomes audible and the floats come into sight, accompanied by the brass players of their initiators, the cheers start. They go very slowly and the applause is rising and waning constantly.

The brass instruments and drums are preceded by majorettes who to me look almost like acrobats. Swinging their huge batons, they throw them high into the air, catch them again skillfully, from time to time jumping onto one shoulder of a male band member, some of them being lifted up onto one hand only.

All of them are dressed in fantasy uniforms, sporting the colors of their school, city or clubs.

For me, it is still a new feeling to "show color and flag". I begin to feel that having been raised in post-war Germany, I was never encouraged to demonstrate belonging, let alone fidelity. Admittedly, during sport competitions of different regions or countries, it was okay, though, to cheer at the victory of your own team. Yet it cannot be compared by far to the depth and warmth which American students are encouraged to show their emotions with. At the same time touched and irritated, I start to wonder what they do when they have to change schools because the family is moving. Is it then state of the art to change sides quite naturally?

I downright laugh aloud when Rob Beverly raises money for a helicopter flight that is to take place over the rival school on the eve of the next football game, flying a banner saying "Three cheers to Azusa! We shall win!"

But Azusa does win. And Rob is as proud as a peacock.

Chapter 14

Six or Sex

After having earned quite a few grins when pronouncing the number "6" close to the German way, I now put some effort into explicitly saying "six". But I am not the only foreigner having problems along that line. There are several jokes around which today in the 21st century would all come under "politically incorrect".

One of the favorites mocks the Asians, their telephone number being: sex sex sex free sex to-night (666 36 28). In 1966 there are by far not as many Asians in Southern California as e.g., in San Francisco and there is no Chinatown in LA. They are recognized for their hardworking and ambitious ways, but despite their low-profile policy, one doesn't yet take them seriously into account.

As far as I am concerned, I have a "sweet accent", but nobody tries his "Come on, Kraut, say "th" on me. Also, clever lines like "Sis gel is frrrom Chemeny" don't work with me, I have an answer ready before they can finish their sentence. Boys like to test my integrative efforts with insider teenage phrases like ABC gum (already been chewed) and I quickly learn to distinguish by their mimics whether to answer unsuspectingly or to just turn away.

"Come on, baby, I love you" is one of their frequent appeasing follow-up phrases, implying my lacking sense of humor. I should have just laughed out loud, okay? I get it and more and more I comply.

Phrases referring to stereotype pictures of Germany I find more difficult to just accept. Sometimes uttered mockingly, at times with tongue in cheek, but rarely also contemptuously. I have my answers ready and with time just stop being annoyed or even hurt. This includes my tolerance of TV series like "Hogan's Heroes" where the Germans in general are depicted as " Yavoll" howling Nazis.

My host sisters are unbelievably fair as far as German-bashing is concerned. Neither my accent nor Germany's latest history are ever mentioned. Relaxed talks with Ann or Kerry are usually about boys. As things go, neither of them is getting the dates they aspire. Ann, for instance, is very tall for a girl. At that time, going out with a boy who was shorter than you, in spite of you wearing shoes with flat heels, would have been the laughing stock. As coincidence wants it, there is a tall handsome boy. Alas, he doesn't react.

Kerry, outgoing and always in a good mood, also has her eyes on a boy she facies. He seems not uninterested in her, either. When the three girls of us stop on a sunny afternoon for a coke at popular Fastfood-Drive-In, guess who soon stops beside us? Well, I'll be darned if it isn't ... And sure enough, he is looking in our direction, grinning charmingly.

Kerry must have been embarrassed because she starts to make nasty remarks. Looking straight ahead, she grumbles:

"You can't hear me, you bloke, but I just can't help telling you that you are not nice. Don't worry, though, we all have our mistakes. Nobody is perfect."

Ann and I break out in unrestrained laughter, Kerry joins in. But not only Kerry, the object of her adoration also is chuckling audibly. His window had been completely open all the time, but Kerry had thought it was pulled up. Ann quickly puts in the rear gear and speeds away.

Kerry is inconsolable:

"What the hell have I done? What on earth did I silly cow say that for? I blew it! I blew everything! That's the end of it! "

Anyway, he did invite her to the next school dance.

I myself like Rob Beverly, but somehow, we never seem to get close enough, in a series of narrow misses. When Ann tells me the hot news that he had asked her at the baseball game where she had left her pretty sister, I feel weak in the knees.

"Who? Kerry?" she had retorted.

"No, Uraine" he had murmured.

But I am turned off immediately when Ann tells me his next line.

"You know, I think she is very sexy".

Although Ann assures me that this was not considered a derogatory remark among teenagers, I can't take it as a compliment.

Then I get another briefing in American dating culture. John P., who had invited me to the Valentine's Dance earlier, was the best friend of Rob. Maybe that could have been a reason for Rob not to openly approach me.

Word spreads around at school that Irene isn't so eager to date. This gives me the opportunity to study and read extensively in the few hours that haven't been planned for ahead of time. My love for literature keeps growing. I learn to appreciate the exquisite sense of humor of Mark Twain's and the flaming plea for justice that runs through the dramas of Tennessee Williams.

Since my other subjects like Government and Home&Family also require reading. American history captures my interest, but manuals for good housekeeping provoke my resignation. Never would I become a perfect homemaker. I couldn't even sew. I hate to shorten my mail-order dresses by hand. In the Sixties, dresses had wide swinging skirts, mind you.

My mom has thought of a special treat for me and invited a young German man for dinner. He is 22 years old and is enrolled as a student at a nearby college. I find him extraordinarily well-behaved and marvel at his perfect manners. He is dressed immaculately in a dark suit, shirt and tie included, even later, when we have our first date.

His name is Klaus Mayer. When at the dinner table in my host family, we try to speak German together. This is an absolute No-Go. Not only my mom, but also my sisters interrupt us and declare this behavior to be extremely impolite. After having tried once more, we have to leave it at that.

On the next day, the postman brings a thank-you card on which Snoopy is seen jumping up high with Charlie Brown applauding. "Thank you!" is written on it in big letters. When we open it, the inside contains increasing thanks and a hand-written note by Klaus Mayer, thanking the family for the nice evening.

"A young gentleman with good manners!" Mom is visibly delighted. Unfortunately, when, coming back home, I tell the family enthusiastically about my first date with Klaus, the fun seems to be over.

What happened? I don't get it. Klaus and I are still on formal terms, addressing each other the formal German way. We had a gorgeous buffet lunch at a hip Los Angeles restaurant. Afterwards he took me to a baseball game of his college's and finally rounded up the day at a vista point high above Los Angeles, where one has a spectacular view of the region and all its flickering lights.

Mom becomes increasingly silent and her face hardens more and more. Then she determinedly announces that I am forbidden to see Klaus again. He supposedly was too old for me and I wouldn't be able to handle him in an emergency (?).

Ann und Kerry inform me as to who was a proper date for me. They also tell me about who at our high school was considered a "fagot" and who was "square".

It is "state of the art" to crack jokes about homosexuals. Moreover, conservative parents are derogatively called "L2".

Soon afterwards, a classmate invites me to see his parents' farm. I find out that he is a genuine cowboy. It really is like in the movies: fenced pastures with many cows grazing, supervised by a number of cowboys on horseback. They all sport leather fringed chaparajos, leather boot with spurs, checkered shirts and the well-known hat.

At a distance, a lengthy cowshed comes into sight. The family has thought of a special treat for my visit. I am lectured that most animals there were actually cows, with some oxen added for the necessary hard jobs. But there was only one bull.

We enter the shed and now comes the surprise. I get to meet the bull, who is presently being led to a mock backside of a cow, made of card-bord paper. This picture is likewise fastened to a fence. My date is guiding the bull towards the image. From the opposite side, another boy is encouraging the bull to come closer. Faster than I can follow what is going on, the bull jumps onto the picture and before long, a farmhand proudly presents a creamy whitish substance to us.

"Got him! Yeah!" sounds his triumphant cry. Everyone is clapping their hands and cheering loud. I remember taking quite a while to apprehend what had happened. Then I recall staring at the straw-covered floor for as long as it was humanly possible.

But now it is dinner-time! The inevitable round grill is dangling from three chains over a substantial metal bowl full with glowing charcoal. It is now adorned with steaks which are so big that one estimated would have been enough to feed half the crew present. I am not very hungry, I find.

Once, when I was sunbathing at Malibu beach with a group of students, three slim, suntanned handsome boys were approaching us. They had surfboards tucked under their arms and were visibly enjoying themselves. The middle one stopped right in front of me, addressing me in a friendly manner:

"Hi there! My name is Brian Wilson, I am a Beach Boy. Want to go out with me?"

Silly girl I was, I retorted mockingly:

"Hi! My name is Irene Schlör, I am an AFSer and no, I don't."

I had all the laughs on my side, but very probably missed an interesting date.

Another nice memory I cherish is of an AFS-outing into the desert. At night, the stars there are not only shing in the sky, they are all around you. And they come in different shades of colors and intensity. It is almost as if you are surrounded by twinkling lights while sitting in the still warm sand. They flare up to your left, to your right, some definitely at a distance, others moving towards you. They come in heaps, in rows, in stripes. It gives you a feeling of being securely embedded in the vastness of the universe. You are almost tempted to move skywards wanting to become a part of this feast.

Chapter 15

AFS

There is a rumor among the AFSers in Southern California which seems to grow wilder as it spreads. After a short time, when the Brasilian exchange student in question is being sent home, it is confirmed.

He is already eighteen and got married to a Californian class mate in Mexico. This was possible because according to Californian law, she was also of age.

The delicacy of the matter is highlighted by the fact that he must have entered Tijuana, Mexico, illegally without a passport. Once there, they must have presented their respective identity documents and could get legally married. She is (of course?) supposed to be pregnant, by the way.

The statutes of the organization which selects and supervises us foreign students, are very clear about serious misconduct. In such a case, the students are to be shipped back home right away. And what happened to the American girl, his legal wife? Why, she just went along with him. And they lived happily ever after? However, many a doubt remains as to how the fairy tale would end.

All participants in the exchange program (which it really isn't, because the family of the student is not expected to host an American teenager on their part) receive very good and extensive care and advice. Not only the AFS headquarter in New York is their constantly available contact, but also regional and local chapters which are all lead by volunteers. It is a matter of prestige to be engaged in AFS charity.

The (female) regional chapter head usually has a home with room to throw parties for 50 up persons.

For this Sunday, we are invited to one of them, host sisters and brothers included. In the morning, we get to try horseback riding. The only prerequisites are solid shoes and long pants. I quickly get the hang of it and my only problem remains galop, I keep on jumping up and down which must look truly ridiculous.

The home that hosts us is large, single level, the way it is customary in California. It is situated on a hill behind extensive orange groves. The entrance area is the first thing to impress the visitor: orange trees to the right and left lining the way, then a little wood, followed by a lawn strewn with avocado trees and leading to a horseshoe-shaped drive-way. The entrance area is laid out with plaster stones, but there are two side doors which are used a lot more frequently. The one on the right side leads directly into the huge kitchen, also serving as a "family room". There is also an adjacent dining room where an endless mahogany table with twelve chairs is visible in the distance. To the right and left, there are six bedrooms with a separate bathroom each.

There is wall-to–wall carpeting everywhere. In the living room, there are French windows which sport a gracious view of the surrounding countryside. The stereo can be adapted individually for every room as well as for the whole house, this feature allowing for a variety of announcements made from the kitchen. The telephones connect to the kitchen by just picking up the receiver.

The Mexican staff comes in the morning by their own cars and park them at the back of the house. They have to bring their own lunch, because meals or even snacks are not part of the hiring conditions.

The mistress of the mansion is avoiding luxury and showing off. She explains her way of shopping to us: only the necessary things, preferably in wholesale centers and, if possible, when they are on a sale. Her three children are raised to be thrifty. The oldest one is also a Senior in high school and presently applying for different summer jobs in order to make some pocket money for the time in college.

Regular meetings in AFS chapter ladies' homes, often in the form of pool parties, offer room for advice or complaint and comparison with other students.

My fellow AFSers come from all countries I can think of right away. Somehow, I get the feeling that South Americans are in the majority. But there are also many Germans, other Europeans, a few from South Africa as well as other African countries, followed by Australians, New Zealanders and Japanese. I cannot remember ever having met any AFSers from beyond the Iron Curtain, neither from India or China.

There are also get-together occasions at different schools. We go into the classes and tell the students about our countries. Usually, the question-answer part after our lecture takes up most of the hour.

Later we are getting feedback – usually positive, sometimes very diplomatically put - from the teachers in question. Classes are reported to have talked among each other extensively about our visits. Soon I realize the big responsibility involved in everything I say in public. Sometimes my statements are all the students ever heard and will know about Germany for a long time to come.

It is not exaggerating to state that here in the USA at the time I witnessed, the general interest in the rest of the world is not very pronounced. Their world begins at the Canadian border and ends at the Mexican one. Simplify your views and attitudes.

Europe, though, is to some extent an exception. Almost all my school mates would like to go on a trip to Europe sooner or later, preferably between high school and college. The essential itinerary they prefer is to see something like six countries in five days. Everybody is convinced that the USA are the navel of the world. In some aspects, there is no doubt about it.

When invited to give a speech at any NGO about my home country, I try to adapt a serious and matter-of-fact tone. This is due to the fact that I want to be listened to and taken seriously. When I notice from the facial expressions of my audience that they couldn't care less or are just listening complacently, I almost feel disrespected.

Some questions force me to stick to the facts, like when they ask whether we have central heating in Germany or running water in the toilets, whether all siblings in a family have to share one bed and it is true that we eat sauerkraut at every meal.

Some questions often recur, e.g. "Why did this guy, what's his name, Hitler, start the war? "

And without any exception, every time they ask:

"How do you like America?"

I honestly do like it here, even if some things catch me by surprise every now and then. this also concerns certain unwritten rules. One of them contains the answer to the question above, the answer to which must be:

"I like it very much. I think it is a great country".

As time goes by, my speeches are getting better. More often now, I get my picture in the local newspapers. Once, upon entering an assembly room, I notice on the wall behind the seat of the president of the club, right next to the club pennant, an enlarged photograph of myself and the reproduction of a newspaper article. I still remember how very embarrassed I felt at that.

Thinking back, my most favorite memory goes to the pleasant atmosphere at a Kiwanis Club. When I learned some days later that they had taken care of my dentist bill, my positive feelings grew even stronger. I had lost a filling in a molar tooth which needed to be taken care of immediately.

American Field Service, this exchange program has originated from a club of volunteers who took care of veterans in the field hospitals and later at home.

In the year 1966 their motto is:

"Walk together, talk together all ye peoples of the earth. Then, and only then shall ye have peace."

For the participating students, this is truly a never recurring chance. they get insight into the real everyday life of the average American family and school life. The host families get some tax reductions for their contributions, but that is usually it. They are supposed to be rewarded with the joys and variety a young foreign member will add to their family.

The vast majority of us AFS students is determined to come back at some time in the near future. They are not allowed to stay on, that is the first condition of their scholarship. The guaranteed return to their home countries is partly to avoid the implication that AFS be a machinery to encourage a "brain drain".

Even the preparatory procedures for the students are every elaborate. I remember having to consult a government certified physician who examined me thoroughly and handed me a health pass classifying me as a member of a certain group. I was also given a slide with an X-ray of my lungs with the order "to guard it like your passport".

My host family told me they had to work their way through a brochure, at the end of which they had to absolve a test. It included questions regarding potential conflict situations and the handling of those:

"If you don't want your guest to use your toothpaste, tell him so".

Towards the end of the year, a bus trip was organized for us students taking us all the way from Southern California up to Western Canada and back to New York. There were roughly 30 participants from over 20 nations assigned to every bus. All of them spoke English, although they might have had a different common mother tongue. The four other students from Germany, Renate, Heinz, Jutta and Regina, all declared unanimously, they couldn't converse in Germany fluently any more. Regina asked to please call her "Reggie" and Hans didn't tire to stress the superiority of the American way, although his accent was even more pronounced than Dr. Ruth Westheimer's.

On this bus trip which lasted almost three weeks, we went from California to Arizona, New Mexico, Oklahoma, Missouri to New York and Canada (just to see the Niagara Falls from the most spectacular angle), staying overnight everywhere at selected families with children our age, the highlight of the journey was in Washington D.C., where we had a gigantic lunch in the garden of the White House, welcomed by President Lyndon B. Johnson and also addressed by Richard Nixon, who was then running for the next presidency. Both of them mingled with the crowd and were careful to shake as many hands as possible.

The next luncheon in the same town was at the German Embassy. We were seated at endless seeming properly laid-out dining tables covered with white table cloths, a fact all of us commented first. We were served beef roulades German style with side potatoes and red cabbage. Most of us were silent and ponding, a few conversed scarcely in German. Luckily enough, the speaker of our delegation, himself the son of a German family of diplomats, saved our honor by giving a flawless table toast to our host. He thanked the German ambassador for his hospitality, the latter then proceeding to introduce his staff, citing all of them by their official titles. This was a strange kind of formality to us, since during the past year we had gotten used to calling everybody by their first names.

Most probably it was the fact that I wrote a letter home almost every day during my exchange year in the USA, which saved me from losing contact with my German upbringings and language. Ever since then, I have often pondered about how easy the AFS year came to exchange students nowadays. They are in constant contact with family and friends over the internet using their mobile phones or laptops.

As always, there are two sides to every fact. Over fifty years ago, we students, because of our very thorough isolation, we were immersed not only in the American language, but became part of the American way of life almost effortlessly. We became more independent and grew up faster. How so? Well, we couldn't run to Mama with every supposedly heartfelt "injustice" and "pain". And when, at the earliest after two weeks, there was an answer to our complaining letter, the "catastrophe" had usually been already forgotten.

Chapter 16

Informal Society?

If one were to judge the Americans according to the way Mr. Cullan teaches, they would seem to be at first sight a very informal society. When in Lit&Comp we had our introductory lesson in German literature, I couldn't resist jotting down a few remarks our teacher made. I then translated them into German and sent them in a letter to my mother.

"Right. This sweet doll by the name of Kriemhild had a crush on this sexpot Siegfried. Well, and then there was this other couple Gunther and Brunhilde. Gunther, this weakling, this patsy, wanted to marry Brunhilde, a true power lady. So, what? She coyly made a fuss of it and played hard to get. She sent out word that she would only marry the man who could beat her in athletics and set up a competition among the playboys of the country. Now you see, Siegfried, Gunther's best friend, was a real superstar in sports. He just put on his magic hood – Who of you doesn't know what a magic hood is? - and whoops, nobody could see him.

What do you think happened then? Why would anyone make himself invisible in a sports competition? Okay, he planned to help his budy Gunther win the event. He wanted to win Brunhilde in matrimony. Mat-ri-mo-ny, don't ever confuse it with har-mo-ny! Right. You go ahead now!

Anymore playing chess? Try and think further than the next move.

– Exactly! She finds out and – well, boys, I sure would have loved to spare us this outcome - she really does it and hangs him onto a nail in the bedroom wall."

Muted giggling is heard among the class, gradually rising to a snort and then an overall general loud neighing which ends in roaring laughter.

But don't get fooled by the relaxed atmosphere. Mr. Cullan knows how to restore order in a wink.

Now, what about formality within the family? Everything easy-going and relaxed? I find out that in some families even today the father is called "Sir" by his children. Thinking about my host family, I remember vividly one characteristic episode. Kerry, my younger guest sister, has an incredibly beautiful voice, an effortless sounding Soprano of the finest kind.

When her music teacher, an opera singer whose house she cleans for about three hours in return for one hour of voice lessons recently told her she was now ready to get instructions from a renowned professor. She would gladly provide contact. However, the professor charges sixteen dollars an hour, almost impossible to afford for any normal person.

One night, we are having another dinner guest, a well-to-do friend of the family. When he tactfully suggests to pay for Kerry's voice lessons, I see my foster dad get angry for the first time. He is still in control of himself when he says quietly:

"Kerry is my daughter and she will only get what we as a family can afford."

No trace of easygoing conversation, but a father's pride and awareness of traditional values can be detected in his overtones.

For another example, let us take the overall important family car of the Sixties. Why do I stress its importance? For one thing, at that time in all of the Greater Los Angeles Area there is almost no public transport system.

Did we copy the Americans or have they imitated us Europeans in this matter? The car is one of the most significant status symbols. In this property, for some people it even comes before the neighborhood area. ("Keeping up with the Joneses").

The cars are designed to impress indeed. When once, after an AFS meeting, the son of the house drives me home in a white automatic 66 model Pontiac Catalina with red leather interior, I am unable to hide my amazement and approval.

In spite of the general speed limit of 90 to 120 (in the desert) miles an hour all over the country, everybody exceeds the allowed rate and thus loves to play with the risk of getting stopped by a howling police car, which can be quite scarry.

After you have stopped, a policeman approaches the driver's window from the back, signaling in arrival for you to turn down the window pane. He briskly asks for your driver's license and vehicle documents. If you behave or sound fresh in any way, they ask you to get out and it takes considerably longer for you to be fined and get your papers back, thus hopefully able to drive on.

So, we are stopped and the policemen are very friendly when they hear that I am a visitor from Europe.

"Germany? Spreken siy doytch?"

"Jawohl, officer", I answer jokingly. "It's all my fault. I was admiring that smart car and in Germany there is no speed limit, as you know, so ..."

"Be on your way, but mind your speed, will you?" The policeman gives us a broad smile and lets us go on.

Whew. That was close.

But we need to return to the subject which predominantly influences teenage culture in the US. A well-known cartoon of the time shows a married couple in front of a telephone which is attached to a wall. ?"The woman is in tears; the man looks truly upset. The line under the caricature goes:

"How could you ever say that our daughter was home on a Saturday evening!"

I myself have witnessed similar remarks. Once I stayed overnight at a classmate's house.

"No daughter of mine goes out of the house without any lipstick on." were her instructions.

Who dates whom? There are unwritten rules regulating this matter as well. Birds of a feather flock together. This means age, social status and looks as well. The popular girl goes out with the sportive guy, the reserved one with the quiet type. If you find or want no one at all, you are dragged on to meet at a blind date. Double dates are also frequently approved of, especially by parents.

It is generally understood that marrying young is the way to go, because extramarital sex would be improper and because a marriage will naturally produce offspring. However, there are in the Sixties quite a number of intellectuals who also encourage girls to go on to college and thus remain single for the next few years.

The desire to enjoy equal rights is already subliminally present in the American society. Within a few years to come, it was to spread like a wildfire.

What about the application of these facts to everyday school life? Are all Seniors constantly focusing on dating? Or is everyone preoccupied with lessons and studying and as for dating, does it just come under further ran?

At Azusa High School for instance, we have sportive and clever Rob. Rob Beverly is the one who collects money among his fellow students in order to let a provocative banner fly over Glendora, the arch rival of the Aztecs. On the day before the first football game, he hires a helicopter, which for half an hour is trailing behind in big letters:

"Azusa Aztecs will crush Glendora Tartans".

He is on the scrounge and spares nobody. The girls he asks to bet him.

"If I win, I'll take you to the movies. If you win, you take me."

Since dating is restricted by tight rules, he is offered money instead. In this way, he manages to collect a sufficient amount to pay for his project.

Rob Beverly's best friend is John P. John is a very good sportsman also, he plays tennis.

While Valentine's Day is almost unknown in Germany during the 60ties, in America it is observed with fervor and almost with passion. Presents are given, especially for girls and women: flowers, chocolates, little cuddly toys. Of utmost importance are greeting cards with all varieties of hearts on them, often accompanied by secret confessions. Who sent you one? And, more important, how many did you get?

On one of my Valentine cards, I find the picture of an angler sitting alongside a river. The text under it goes:

"Nothing fishy about this line, you are a real sweet Valentine".

When John is the first one to ask me to the Valentine's dance, according to prevailing customs I have to accept. Since everything concerning anyone's dates is first-rate gossip and travels fast, it would have been equal to political suicide not to accept. And as for John, he is a nice guy, no doubt about that.

For that occasion, I need to wear a long dress, matching gloves and high heels. A visit to the hair stylist is also mandatory, my hairdo must look properly teased as high as possible.

John has to wear a white dinner jacket, under which goa a white shirt and a tie.) He will sport black trousers and black leather shoes, the kind that is tied with shoe laces. He is supposed to further pick me up from home bringing along a corsage of flowers (neither white nor red). This floral arrangement can be up to one foot long and must be either pinned on the left upper side of your dress or alternatively worn on a clasp on your upper arm. The clasp comes with it, so I manage to fix mine, made up of yellow carnations and tiny yellow roses, on my left arm.

John almost didn't recognize me when I welcomed him formally. Perplexed, he looked at my host mother and Kerry as if asking for confirmation of my identity. I was all made-up and dressed up, the way it was supposed to be.

Mom is glad and proud, because she has sewn my fancy formal.

On our way to the dance, we drop by family Beverly, where Rob and his girlfriend are waiting for us. Mrs. Beverly has insisted she make Polaroid photos of the four of us before we leave. Bob's girlfriend is sporting a real tower of a hairdo. They would have to let down the top of the car, I reckon. Unfortunately, when we are all set, grinning widely into the camera, it goes on strike. Not even the third try with a new film will work. John suggests, we drop by his parents and have them take our photograph.

When we finally arrive at the ballroom, everybody admires my outfit and looks, causing me to become vain and outgoing. Very few people, let alone young ones, can resist a shower of compliments. I find myself entertaining the whole table.

John is visibly proud of me, jokingly calling me "Wienerschnitzel", "Volkswagen" and "little Sauerkraut" alternately.

After some time, John clears his throat and addresses me in front of the whole crowd:

"Airena, I love you."

"How nice of you, John."

"Want to marry me?"

"Sure", I say jokingly. John remains undeterred.

"We could go to Las Vegas. You could say, you were 18. And then you would be an American citizen, nobody could take you back to Germany, and we would be married."

Although all we had to drink was alcohol-free fruit cocktails, I suddenly start to feel hot. Probably, I also blushed on top of it.

Our fellow table mates now turn their whole attention to us.

"What are you two whispering over there?"

"What kind of ring is this on your finger, Irene?" That comes from Maggie.

"My grandmother gave it to me for my Confirmation when I was 14." That is the truth.

"Do all German grandmothers give their grandchildren engagement rings?" That is Rob Beverly.

Laughter from all sides.

"Tell that to your grandmother!"

Around ten thirty, most of the couples proceed to leave the venue in order to go for a fancy supper.

John is in any extraordinarily good mood and starts to talk mockingly about "Junior", calling me "wifey". When it dawns upon me that our fictive future son is meant by that, it is almost too late.

"Stop the nonsense, John, or else I'll never talk to you again!" These magic words finally do the trick.

At the end we head for home, passing by the Beverlys again, where Mrs. Beverly, a truly fine lady, admonishes John to take me home right away without any further delay.

My host sister Kerry, too, is having problems with dating. Not that she is madly in love with David whose mother, however, is giving them hell. As soon as after their first date, she put a newspaper clipping on her son's bed, awaiting him as soon as he returned. The big headline read: 16-year-old pregnant by 13-year-old boyfriend.

Mothers and their admonishing! My own mother has just answered my enthusiastic letter describing the Valentine's Ball. She sounds as if I expected illegitimate twins, to say the least. "Illegitimate" was a disgrace back in 1966.

In the second half of the Sixties, we experienced the sexual revolution which has turned everything upside down. However, in the US, marriage never went out of fashion like it soon after did in Europe. To have a child outside of marriage has remained a flaw, if not a blemish. The only exception is maybe granted to movie actors and popular singers.

Chapter 17

Life goes on

My grandma Emma has died. It says so in the obituary announcement, which my mother had cut out from our local newspaper "Heilbronner Stimme" and sent to me along with her letter.

My dear wife, our loyal mother, mother-in-law and grandmother, Emma Schlör née Hilberger, has died at the age of 66.

This is about my grandma, no doubt. How can she just die away when I'm not there and I won't even be able to even attend her funeral?

I wrangle over fate.

It's not fair to be left out. Will I really never see her again then? She always let us go to the bakery and buy pretzels and bagels and donuts when we visited. Grandpa used to fetch a bottle of homemade fruit juice from the cellar and take us to the garden, where the chicken coop stood at the very end. We carefully picked up a few eggs and took them to Grandma's kitchen, where the window was open and a dark brown spiral of adhesive tape dangled from the ceiling, getting darker and darker with time, as more flies stuck to it.

Grandpa? What will grandpa do without grandma? He always asked her before he did anything, even like should he put on his sturdy shoes or not. Grandpa still has a cartridge in his skull from the First World War. We have seen it many times on the huge x-ray that he used to hold against the window. The big white space which can be seen above the bullet, is a silver plate, which Grandpa also has in his skull. Ever since the First World War.

Grandpa is not sick. He rides his NSU Quickly motorbike all over Weinsberg till it rattles. But he calls his wife "Mommy", as all his sons do. Grandpa without grandma?

"What's the matter? - Oh, no! " Kerry now looks at the newspaper clipping that had slipped from my hand and dropped on the floor.

"That's your last name! Who is it? "

She suggests a walk would do us good now. This is very untypical in a country like California. Nobody goes anywhere without a meaningful purpose. Even jogging in the street was still not very common at that time either.

We walk through the streets of the neighborhood for about an hour, until little brother Mike catches up with us on his bike and tells us we were supposed to come home for dinner.

"Now, how was that for therapy?" Mom asks and looks at me compassionately, though still doubtfully.

It actually did me good. I feel refreshed and calmed down. After eating and washing up with my sisters, I even sit down to study for the next day, because we have a Midterm Exam in Government.

The next morning, I am looking at Mr. Clark with unconcealed dislike as he hands out the exam papers. They contain an estimated 200 questions. I am positive that they will cover just about everything he went through in class.

"How are you doing, Irene?" he asks scornfully as he passes by me again after about an hour.

"Just skip the questions you are not sure about. You can always go back again after you have finished. "

I am all worked up and misunderstand his remarks, taking them for an advice to hurry up. I anxiously start to write again. Mr. Clark's exams are not only made up of multiple-choice questions, but also ask for essay-type statements.

And what will Mrs. Schelling say if I'm late for my upcoming French lesson? My French teacher back home in Germany, Dr. Heyn, has sent me a textbook which I comes in handy when I need to look up something. I really enjoy learning languages, and because of my solid background in Latin, I easily catch even sophisticated English vocabulary coming from Romance languages. The more I read, the more I understand that the English language is full of them.

My grandmother Emma called the ceiling "Plafond", the sidewalk "trottoir" and the neighbor was living " vis-a-vis ". Grandpa got us apple cider from the "souterrain" and instead of "these and those" he said "die und selle". There were no Anglicisms in their language, no ticket and no event, no teenagers and not even lunch.

"I don't know why you are all worked up," my mother writes in her letter of reply to my lamentations. "Old people are dying. She was your grandma, I understand that, but on the other hand, she never liked me, your mother, because I was a foreigner. She also preferred you to your sister because you have brown eyes like almost all members of the Schlör family. She was very narrow-minded, you know. "

In other letters I read about the great number of mourners who gave Grandma Emma the last escort. Suddenly, my point of view changes and I start to look at things not just as being in a different place, but also in a distant time.

I could see all those philistines at the funeral, dressed in black, shedding a tear or two and dropping their flowers into the grave. Afterwards there would be coffee and cakes, also sandwiches and alcoholic beverages during the past-funeral gathering. The possible cause of grandmother's death would be discussed uninhibitedly, muffled and behind hands over mouths at first, then more and more openly and in front of more and more listeners.

"Apparently she has pushed back herself the oxygen tent over her hospital bed."

"She had cancer of the colon."

"Do you know why there were so many people in the cemetery? She used to be with 'Mother and Child'. Wore the Mother's Cross herself."

Shouldn't I rather stay in America? Or at least apply to one of the American universities? But where at?

It does not seem to interest my fellow students that there are also other states in the USA apart from California. Institutions like MIT (Massachusetts Institute of Technology), Harvard and Yale are of course known, but "back East" instead of "out West", thus of little concern.

Good people are always wanted, so the Department of Education of the government organizes inter-country college entrance exams and even individual exams in various subjects, where a very good result almost equates a scholarship in the corresponding field.

However, good sportsmanship is the greatest asset a candidate can have. A good athlete is accommodated at almost every university and is also bound to graduate. That's just how things work over here.

Where did the descendants of grandma Emma's brother Otto go to school? Did he have any?

Grandma Emma sometimes used to talk about him. He emigrated to America and wrote just two letters home from there. One day, years later, their mother Mina reportedly just straightened herself abruptly and murmured with an absent look in her eyes:

" Now my boy has died."

Chapter 18

A Rolling Stone Gathers no Moss

The American attitude towards heath is remarkable. Resting in bed during illness is just about the worst thing to do. Consequently, children with minor ailing are sent to school.

The belief in two Aspirins and half a liter of orange juice a day being the universal remedy and preventing any impending contagion is firm and undisputed. Persons feeling sick should be encouraged to get busy with any chores in order not to concentrate on their diseases.

With time, I have adopted this view without really noticing I did. Meanwhile, I am convinced that it is helpful at least when feeling blue and having a depression. As for orange juice, I cannot stand the smell of it any more, let alone the taste.

At the end of February 1966, California is hit by a severe flu epidemic. Many schools close, yet not the ones in the comparatively poorer communities. As it happens, they do not get government support for every day they are closed. This is why Azusa High School students are at that time fighting red noses, swollen eyes and sore throats.

When somebody gets injured, only heavily bleeding wounds are tended to. Otherwise, it is concerned better to not disinfect and bandage it. Just leave it alone, it will take care of itself, is the implication. Even fractures are just put in a splint, but disuse of the limbs is nevertheless discouraged. Lying down and resting are associated with succumbing to creeping death. Whether freshly operated or just out of the delivery room, the rule is to get back to normal as soon as possible.

Complaining and whining is as good as unknown, it is just not tolerated. Consolation is offered only in the form of standard phrases. When a person bemoans something, he is asked to analyze the situation as in reference to himself. What did he contribute to the condition getting worse and coming to this point? All in all, one is expected to treat one's body and also time responsibly.

The classical Greek definition of tragic, which is to have been punished by fate although being innocent, does not apply any more here out West.

When considering this philosophy, it is easier to understand that health insurance and old age pensions are mainly seen as one' s private affair.

Disabled people, on the contrary, are being helped and supported; they are taken seriously.

The common belief concerning health includes the fervent defense of hygiene in all matters. I am truly impressed by the consequent way my American fellow students and everybody else I meet are always freshly showered and dressed in clean clothes. Even the dressing rooms in the gym smell just clean.

There are other precautions like no shaking hands or keeping away from your conversation partner at an arm's length which I imitate automatically. Very soon, I also drink water from public fountains by just pressing a button and keeping my mouth away from the faucet.

And what do the Europeans make out of it? Americans are supposed to be over-all sterile and afraid of touch. Banning every kind of human smell and touch, they were also killing interhuman natural behavior and warmth.

From my experience, I can only say, this does not come anywhere near the truth.

Maybe this belief is due to the envy of people who would like to be Americans or else it is the scorn of the presumable preservers of the Old World? The attitude of 19th century Romantics which puts spirituality over practicality is still going strong among Europeans.

However, philosophy and literature in the States are deemed more important in education than is generally known in Europe. Although films are preferred to books, their quality and impact should not be underestimated. Hollywood is not only a place where fairy tales and dreams are produced for the consolation of underdogs and wallflowers, likewise not only a trendsetter of other movie industries, but also offers serious discussion of universal human problems. Films are not inferior to books, like Europeans generally rush to claim, but they offer possibilities to critically review one's own life and present insight to questions of justice – on a different level than books do.

In the same way a picture can convey more than a thousand words, a motion picture can bring to life in a short time what generations of philosophers have been gathering in centuries. Not necessarily, but possibly.

Considering European movies, one observes that e.g., the French "film noir" is not popular at all with Americans. After all, optimism is a central pillar of American philosophy.

Magazines and newspapers are printed and sold in abundance. The papers are full of critical, opinion-forming and thus influential articles, representing American culture.

Ernest Hemingway is one of the writers cultivating simplicity of insight. He wrote many short stories, tales with momentous content. Hemingway is in a way an example of a sort of European-American synthesis. His style is bare of frills, no emotions are elaborated on, though usually unforeseen action disturbs and changes the lives of his protagonists. The comprehensibility of situations touches his readers profoundly. In a way, he can be called a pacifist and hedonist as well, thus reaching many universal readers.

He once claimed that he hated safe and secure sex. In his understanding, sex should be spontaneous and dirty. In that, no average American would ever agree with him.

Chapter 19

Call of the Wild

Calico Ghost Town is the name of a tourist attraction in the middle of the Californian desert. When I say desert, it doesn't mean camels and sand, but a monotone landscape with encrusted soil of an almost white color. Here and there, bushels of very dark green waxlike plants stick out, none of them very tall, among them also cacti. Barren hills look like bald men's heads from afar.

It is hot. That is why Jutta and her foster sister and Ann and I are traveling in an air-conditioned Chrysler, driven by Chris, the son of a chapter head, on our way to attend an AFS weekend in Barstow. The endless seeming asphalt road is dead straight, looking as if leading into nowhere. Driving is easy and smooth. For quite a number of miles, the boy switches to tempo mat, taking his hands off the steering wheel. The car is gliding on as if in slow motion, though the speedometer tells another tale. In the desert, there is practically no speed limit, which is the greatest thing imaginable for a young male American driver.

The radio loudspeakers (Quadro sound, the latest invention in the field) blare out country music. The carload is thrilled. A common feeling of good vibrations (fun!) unites us and we are "turned on" in the true sense of the word. Chris is having the time of his life with four girls flirting with him.

He starts telling Volkswagen jokes. Jutta and I exchange one quick glance before we join the common cascades of laughter. The scenery offers nothing spectacular. Chis says, they shoot all cowboy movies around here (Wow!) And atomic bombs were fired from this area as well. Chris doesn't say this, but we learned it later, when gossiping among the AFSers.

Los Alamos in Spanish means "The poplars". Does it? There are trees? We are not going to go there for sure. No place for nice AFSers who are supposed to look on the bright side only. It is not in California anymore, anyway. It is in New Mexico.

On this sunny Saturday in March, our meeting point is at the entrance to Calico, a ghost town restored the way it had been before it was abandoned after the gold rush in the middle of the 19th century. Everything looks authentic. The barber's shop which also served as the dentist's, the semi-detached wooden houses of the former inhabitants, the infamous saloon, with swinging doors and veranda. When all the digging and washing brought no yield any more, the caravan moved on.

This story reminds me of the share croppers of today. In California, you can observe them moving from South to North, harvesting oranges, grapes, maize and nuts. They admittedly are a little better off than they were during the time of John Steinbeck, who gave us a vivid picture of their dire nomadic life in "The Grapes of Wrath". In simple, clear and effective language he demounted the myth of the American Dream which in fact applies to the strong and assertive only.

However, this is a bad comparison, I soon realize. The gold diggers moved on out of determination to make their luck after all. The harvest hands move on because they have lost the power to develop any personal initiative.

After Calico, we get on the comfortable bus to head for one of the last Indians' (native Americans) reserves. By the way, nowadays the correct term is Indigene Americans. Political correctness is to make up for discrimination. In some states, it is already forbidden that children play Cowboys and Indians. Even painted faces and feathers as head dress are frowned upon.

What about them, really? The original inhabitants of America have mingled with the influx of migrants after the so-called discovery by Columbus. That is the official version. Popular examples cited are Joan Baez or Cher. Nevertheless, there are still some reserves given to the ones who want to preserve their culture and live the way their ancestors have. When we stop at such a place, we are greeted at the entrance by a real chief in full costume. For a dollar we can have our picture taken with him. He has got such a sad look in his eyes that I ponder for quite some time over why he is succumbing to his role.

The highlight of this densely packed weekend trip is the NASA-Basis Goldstone. The aviation station and space basis leave a lasting impression on us AFSers from all over the world. Not even our mathematically gifted boys can follow everything the guides in different places tell us about. This is probably due to the fact that only selected registered groups are allowed there. The engineers leading us around seem like they were out of this world. Their jargon is full of complicated technical terms and the words "millions" and "billions" are heard frequently. Taking photographs is officially forbidden.

On Sunday night there is a talent show. After church and lunch, we are given half a day to prepare our performance.

We Germans are the biggest group. We decide to rehearse songs which I will accompany on the guitar. "Wir lieben die Stürme", "Trink, trink, Brüderlein trink" and for a final good-bye: "Auf Wiedersehen". To make it more interesting, we decide that every one of us introduce himself, explaining where from he comes and what his home country is like. Experience has taught me that most faces will light up at the mention of "from an area between Heidelberg and the Black Forest".

We are a smashing success. The students from Argentina and from New Zealand also receive a big applause. Alfredo plays a tango on the piano; Maggie swings her hips wearing a bikini top and straw skirt; Steven from South Africa cracks jokes like a professional entertainer:

"My claim to fame is the ability to vegetate". Or:

"In South Africa, mothers tell their daughters never to marry a Catholic, a Jew or someone who can't write his name." The audience is rolling on the floor.

Whoever has invented "political correctness"? Today, over fifty years later, such jokes would be an absolute no-go, not only in Germany. Even the job classification of "entertainer" is something Germans cannot really define. It would range between clown, buffoon, jester, presenter.

In the Sixties in California, it seems, we met almost exclusively happy, enterprising, patriotic people. Not smiling, not joking was definitely considered un-American.

Chapter 20

That's the way the cookie crumbles

Kerry, my younger host sister, has got an engagement as a background singer with a popular band. She has got permission from the principal to go on with it as long as it will not interfere with her school work. At the dinner table, she sometimes shares her experience with us.

The background singers practically carry the performance, she states. All of them are better than the lead vocals, but they must never try to be either eye catcher nor stand out audibly. Their most important feature is to be synchrony. This also includes height, weight, dress, hair and mimics. they must remember being backdrop only, preferably in the semi-dark. If they are too handsome or too loud, they get fired.

That was new to me. I marvel at the clever deception the audience is subject to.

In these days, I am suffering from the compulsion to lose weight. Kerry and I both have a sweet tooth and together we decide to become slim now. Mom complies and serves less desserts and unfortunately, less tasty food. I understand for the first time that rich food accounts for most of the deliciousness. And, by the way, sugar makes you happy. Yes, it does.

Kerry suggests to secretly go to the ice-cream parlor, eat to our hearts' delight and then go to the ladies' room and throw up. If anyone should say anything, we could always claim that the ice-cream didn't agree with our stomachs.

"Just put a finger down your throat".

This asks for quite some willpower. My third try is a success, but I have made a complete mess of the toilet seat.

"Oh no! You were supposed to put your head way down into the toilet bowl!"

The smell of it has permeated her cabin, too, and she rushed over to me.

No. I will not do this again. To clean up such a mess is the height of disgust. I could have slapped my own face. I'd rather gain weight than do that again.

When we arrive at home, Ann (slim as a willow and always in a good mood) looks at us and wrinkles her nose. Then she mockingly wants to know from which Rodeo we were coming back.

The next day, in my Home&Family class I ask my teacher Mrs. Kaymen for her advice. What should I do to lose weight permanently in a healthy manner? This turns out to be a bad idea. She takes it as a hint at her own obesity.

Soon after, I forget my worries about weight. So many other important things come up and demand my attention.

One day towards the end of April, a loudspeaker announcement interrupts our lesson at Azusa High.

"Will all teachers and students please proceed to the gymnasium and take their seats in the previously allocated area. Remember that high heels are not allowed due to the damage they do to the parquet floor."

Obediently, we are trotting towards the gym, glad about unexpected cancellation of our class.

The gym is dimmed. Only a few lights are on. Curiously, we are looking at the lectern with its microphone visible on one of the seat rows, waiting for a speaker. the gym floor itself is empty.

All of a sudden, the spotlight presenting the lectern is on and a female voice starts to sing:

"Moon river, wider than a mile, I'm crossing you in style someday."

Softly, almost hesitatingly, the low voice sings on, without being accompanied by any instrument. Becoming louder and sounding more and more determined, the beautiful soprano voice carries on, as clear as a bell. It is Kerry's voice we are listening to.

"Moon river and me" she ends her song in style.

Enchanted and still a little bewildered, the first listeners start to applaud. The clapping gets louder and turns into an unprecedented cheer, ending only when the principal Mr. Merell mounts the lectern and raises a hand. Everybody is eager for the next song. but instead, Merrell announces with a tint of pride in his voice:

"This song was presented to you by your fellow student Kerry V."

In order to forestall another rise of applause, he adds quickly:

"You may now step down on the floor and dance to the music."

Immediately, the loudspeakers blare out music and we students rush noisily onto the dance floor. The next twenty minutes are all ours. the all-over mood is great.

Although I cannot see Kerry any more, I feel awfully glad for her. Indeed, her self-esteem received a great boost from this wise move of our principal. I gather, the secret of successful pedagogy is actually to get out the best of every student.

Chapter 21

Somewhere, my love

Though Lara has matured, she still is very beautiful. Her blonde hair she has pinned together at the back of her head into a classic chignon. Her features have hardened. She is looking straight ahead and walking briskly through a crowd at a busy crossing. But when the camera swings to the next setting, the audience is taken by surprise;

Jury! Yes. No doubt, it must be him- Well, hasn't he ever aged! Omar Sharif, the best-looking actor of the Sixties, now has greying temples and there are dark circles under his eyes. His lips is slightly parted and he almost gives one the impression of a man suffering from shortness of breath. One almost feels sorry for him. He is almost dragging himself forward, having difficulty keeping up. But all of a sudden, he starts to speed up. Not that he is walking faster, he is panting hard and almost shambling through the crowd. It is almost unbearable to watch him straining himself.

He has spotted Julie Christie alias Lara and starts to croak her name despite his hoarse voice. Yet she just keeps on walking impassively. How can she possibly not hear him or see him?

The whole cinema is suffering with him, no, praying fervently for a happy end.

However, Lara is now mounting a streetcar and settling herself in a window seat, with her features showing no emotion. Jury sees her and starts to run, pressing his hand on his chest.

"Lara, Lara!" his lips are forming her name.

The tram is starting to move now. Doctor Shivago drags himself on for a few steps before he falls to the ground, lifeless now.

Meanwhile, the music is repeating the leitmotiv for the last time and the movie has come to an end.

All the girl students are in tears. The boys seem to be lost in thought.

Is this what happens when you marry a woman you don't really love? However, the focus seems to be on the opening scene of the film with Lara's and Shivago's daughter telling the story of her being abandoned in a crowd by Lara's mate of that time.

"He let go of my hand!" The young woman with the big blue eyes has tear in her eyes as she recalls that moment. She is the frame narrator of the epic.

Does she more look like her mom or her dad, what do you think? The deception is so credible that the students forget they have just seen an entirely fictitious movie with performing actors.

As the students slowly leave the theater, the comments seem to be endless with the audience reliving one touching scene after the other. Nobody is lining up for another popcorn helping.

"I liked best when he cried at the letter from his wife!"

"By the way, what was Lara doing when Zhivago met her again after he was already married?"

"Ironing sheets, you dupe"?"

"Ironing what?"

"What was that ugly old man trying to do with the hose?"

"He pumped out the stomach of his former lover who had tried to commit suicide because he had seduced her fifteen-year-old daughter."

"Ehhh"

"Wasn't that cool when they travelled to their country estate in that freight wagon?"

"And all because of the Commies."

"See how many suitcases Geraldine Chaplin brought back from Paris to Moscow?"

"Yeah, but Zhivago didn't marry her because she was rich."

"He did, too!"

"You stupid moron, you don't even get the gist of a movie!"

Anna is completely in her element now. She was the one who had written to the movie theater and asked for reduced ticket for the eagerly awaited and widely promoted movie about Russia. All Seniors of Azusa High should see that important time documentary, she had stated they would profit a lot by learning the truth. This would prepare them for the future as well.

Anna got the tickets and Juniors and Seniors alike went to the movie theater together. There was no chaperone teacher accompanying them and there were no misfits trying to ruin the event. Obviously, the film touched and fascinated them alike.

Regardless of the professional excellence of the directing and making of the motion picture in general, there were really two major universal themes being touched: extramarital affairs and evil rebels.

At that time, we didn't get the gist of it, we were only influenced profoundly ande rather subconsciously. Neither Effi Briest nor Madame Bovary (Shivago's female counterparts) were known to us. The very professional acting, the transfer of latent or blunt eroticism which the camera managed superbly as well as the breathtaking shooting of the scenery impressed everyone alike.

As soon as I am back in my room, I start to write an enthusiastic criticism of the movie and send it to my family in Germany. Unfortunately, over there this motion picture took several more months to come into vision, impatiently awaited by my grandmother on my mother's side.

Meanwhile, it did serve its purpose in the USA. The common agreement of regarding Communist Russia as their arch enemy was triumphantly reconfirmed.

Chapter 22

Differences

Time for our semester report cards.

We have worked hard for our grades. In two courses of our choice, we had to hand in a paper as well. We had been allowed to choose our own topics.

But the requirements were the same for every subject: Look up your topic in books in three libraries; note the titles, publishers, authors and dates of publication on handy cards, on the back of which you write the appropriate chapters and pages you are going to refer to or quote. Then proceed to write a temporary outline of your paper. Finally write your chapters, correct them and hand in a typed version of around 20 pages.

And that is what we did. All these steps were supervised and commented by our teachers and this way, we had to earn the corresponding credit points.

I feel almost melancholic when thinking of the 1995+ generation of "copy-pasters". Not that there is much to argue against getting things done quickly and efficiently. But then, if you do everything that way, obviously you won't remember and learn much. Honestly, what is the meaning of doing it, if you forget it right afterwards?

My subjects for my semester papers are Lit & Comp and Government. I can score points with "Charles Dickens as a Social Critic". However, my paper on "History of the American Civil War" is not really the runner, although when working on it, I learned more about it than by reading "Gone with the Wind". I remember being all worked up about the taxation of their colony by the English in the 18th century. Actually, the Yankees had to pay extra import taxes to the British when ordering tea from India. Mind you, they weren't having the tea sent to England, but to their own country. As far as I remember, that was the first time I began to realize that money doesn't always go to the one who earns it

Meanwhile, in Home & Family we are all pregnant now. Giving birth is not difficult, we are getting spinal anesthesia and suffer no pain. In the

Germany of the Sixties of the last century, most doctors and people in general held the view that a woman was to suffer at childbirth, thus making the event memorable. Moreover, in no case pain killers were really advised, thus enabling the individual to mature by learning to endure pain. On top of it, God alone knew why he inflicted pain. And black humor stated a person to thus be able to differentiate well-being from illness.

In order to get this message through to the sick and suffering, all possible consequences of suppressing pain and aches were pointed out in a pseudo-scientific manner. In the following decades, several press campaigns were launched against the most frequently used pain killers. To illustrate their detrimental side effects, some rare medical cases of recorded damage were cited. No voices were heard arguing that the benefits should be weighed against the damages.

The fact that in the 21st century comparatively more drug addicts are noted among patients is traced back to complex reasons and cannot serve as an argument to let everybody suffer. As so often, the dosage actually counts.

In many different aspects, Europe was then way behind the U.S. in the development of medical progress. German surgeons would remove infected tonsils as a treatment, snake bites were cured by sucking up the poison and spitting it out; amputated arms and legs often not replaced by artificial ones. In the age of the internet, however, every doctor all over the globe can inform himself about the latest findings in medicine. The only obstacle that might stand in the way of a new treatment seems to the the ethical one.

Coming back the requirements of the Home & Family course, the trend of fifty plus years ago was to raise the students' awareness towards the opposite sex by sanctioning sexual activity in marriage only. In this way, more offspring was provided for, ideally combined with the mutual caretaking of different generations.

But the sexual revolution of the late Sixties turned everything upside down. Foremostly, sex was no longer considered a taboo subject and not confined to one partner any more. General acceptance of extra-marital children followed, resulting in the celebration of individual freedom in all shades and shapes. Oddly enough, this development has turned out more consequent and far-reaching in Europe, not in the U.S., where it had begun.

Do we detect a return to conservativism in the 21st century? The wheel of history might not be turning back, although at times it does wiggle and lag. The Age of Globalization has caught many people unaware and the generally accepted trend of "anything goes" overwhelms and unsettles not only the elderly.

Summing it up by returning to Home & Family, the class definitely was designed to prepare us girls for an upcoming marriage. Actually, about one third of the class was already engaged and intending to get married soon after their graduation.

The rest of the group though, announced their willingness to go on studying, struggling for information and support to proceed in that direction. They didn't really get much encouragement from any side, since a girl's college education was still considered "unamerican".

More than once we played the game "Where I see myself in ten years' time". We were even asked to predict the future of our fellow students. Nobody really objected openly.

Chapter 23

Art or Kitsch?

For Easter Service 1066 the whole family V. are assembled at the church of their denomination. Over the altar I can see a huge picture of Christ crucified, embedded in roses and surrounded by putti. The halo over his head lights up in regular intervals. From a stereo, subdued soul music is heard.

The bigger part of the congregation looks at the slide projection with due respect and even awe. But some tongue-in-cheek glances also cannot escape the scrutinizing observer. The children look on with their eyes wide open.

Being a 17-year-old teen, I scorn the kitsch of the installation. Nothing I had ever been taught before could have justified or even explained it. Unfortunately, what is due to my half-knowledge and lack of maturity, gives most of the people present the impression of my being conceited and arrogant.

Why should things be of lesser value just because our own tradition has taught us to reject them? Admittedly, people do need values to which they can refer in order to establish an identification. These values and backgrounds need to be taught, no question. They become crucial when we live in a family, in a society where we need to harmonize and basically agree in order to continue the togetherness. Nevertheless, our values must not lead to rejection or even despise of other views.

The term kitsch is originally an onomatopoeia term for to glue or to smear. It is unanimously used in a derogatory manner for sweet-sentimental products of a mislead kind of taste, for a kind of pseudo-art, for trash and rubbish, for tries at emotional exploitation.

On grounds of being all-exclusive, this very lofty definition is being questioned now in the 21st century.

What used to be indisputably good and real for the longest time, is now being shaken, faltering like other unquestionable values which had been agreed upon as standard. Since kitsch very early became associated with greedy commerce, the real thing, pure art, was free from being tradeable, available for money or on demand. Part of this 18th/19th century definition lay in the history of European art, for a long time confined to sacral manifestations.

So, is there no difference between art and kitsch? We have today the opportunity to observe art and commerce in never before existing harmony. By definition, art is also expected to move us emotionally (docere et delectare), it is becoming increasingly difficult to detect the difference. Admittedly, there are experts who define some crucial factors, even globally. But in my opinion, they must not be dogmatic or binding. Moreover, we can see how vulnerable definitions really are and how so dependent on their specific period of time and place of origin, when we consider the current view which narrows down art to anything minimalistic.

I believe the same is true for the movement "L'art pour l'art", which narcissistically claims art to be exclusively the realm of artists, allowing just for the appreciation of insiders. My strongest argument against this would be that very few artists want to keep their works to themselves. Art intends to be noticed, to be understood and recognized. On the other hand, we also notice the abuse of art as a way to manipulate the masses.

Docere et delectare – this old definition of art has never lost its validity. Between these two poles it keeps on swinging.

Now, what does this mean for religious art in America? Thinking of churches in California, I didn't get the impression that it really mattered there. Even cemeteries rather look like parks than like places of remembrance and insinuating spiritual reunification in another life.

I recall, however, being surprised when I first saw the small, originally true restored medieval church at the famous cemetery Forest Lawn. According to English originals, it was built from natural stones with gothic style pointed arches and colorful leaded glass windows. They say, it was shipped over from England, stone by stone, and assembled true to life in California. Talking about the country of unlimited possibilities.

In Forest Lawn the graves are level with the ground, no boundaries or decorative flower beds either: Just grass and flat memorial plaques honor the deceased and buried.

So, on Easter Sunday the family and I are sitting in this little church on single chairs each which are comfortably upholstered. Below our feet there is floor carpeting, the ceiling above us is flat. It is commonly agreed that temples, churches and places of reverence are supposed to inspire awe. California is rather pragmatic in that case like in many others. While in New England the churches, even the university halls are designed to communicate tranquility and respect, in the churches in California this is certainly not being transmitted. The clerics, priest and choir, though, are all dressed in gowns.

The episcopalian minister looks somewhat confused. His eyes are sort of glassy, he seems to mumble his words.

Since the congregation pays for their own clerics on a voluntary basis, most churches can't afford to be picky about them.

"He is doing really well. We are so proud of him" means in America that someone has a long way to go in order to get accepted.

Besides the Catholic Church, there are countless groups of Protestant denomination. Protestants are divided also regarding wealth and position.

After church service, there always is an informal stand-up gathering in the yard. Improvised counters provide the congregation with coffee in paper cups and pieces of cake.

"You know, my wife always volunteers for church work. – Oh, so does mine. Absolutely."

"Wasn't that a lovely slide for the occasion? – You bet! Whose idea was that? – Oh, it's all done by Mrs. Miller, she is a true artist. And she arranged for the donuts as well."

"What is your secret recipe, Linda? – Come on, it's a ready-made baking mixture. – Fabulous, like in the commercial: so fluffy you can cut it with a feather!"

"Talking about commercials, did you see Brenda's hair? She must have decided that blondes have more fun. – Do you think so? It could also have come from going to the beach. After all, this is April. The kids won't miss a day of surfing and swimming. They are at Laguna Beach more often than not."

"Well, we'd better be off now. Happy Easter!" – "Praise the Lord!"

Chapter 24

Young and Adventurous

Ann wants to travel around Europe for one month and spend no more than 500 dollars. She has found a travel agency which is organizing a bicycle tour through seven countries. The candidates should be physically top fit and be able to carry with them shirts and shorts of polyester material, a raincape, cooking gear and a one-man tent.

I am trying to talk her out of it, telling her it would be a lot more expensive than she calculated. Staying at youth hostels was not really cheap and food wasn't free either. Besides, the weather was a risk factor. What if she got sick? Ann is developing some sort of defiant behavior whenever the subject comes up.

Since her other plans for the near future include applying for a scholarship at one of the better universities, she is busy for the greater part of the day. Mom and Dad say they won't give her a cent for her studies if she was able to go to Europe for one month on her own money, earned through babysitting and other odd jobs.

So, most of the time, I am together with Kerry. Ann usually goes to bed after we do and, in the morning, she is always the first one in the bathroom. Mom complains if our beds aren't made properly or if we neglect our kitchen chores.

None of us ever has a date any more. We are hectically busy, the grade report due at the beginning of June is going to determine our further career, if nothing else.

We Seniors have already received our school rings. they are gold plated with a blue stone in the middle and the writing "Azusa" on it. It is embedded in a miniature emblem. To the right and left side of this, our initials are placed on the picture of an ornate Aztec warrior. The girls have smaller rings than the boys and they put them on their right hand, "because someone might give you a different ring for your left hand".

The boys have really chunky editions of the same rings. When a boy and a girl "go steady", they exchange their rings. Girls then usually wear the huge type of ring dangling on a necklace around their neck. Fervent Azusa

High fans have yet another choice of showing their loyalty. The "Senior Keys" are chains, an amulet version of the Senior rings.

However, this is only the beginning of Senior privileges. More is to come: At the end of the school year there will be an XXL version of a ball, the "Seniors' Prom ".

But the twelfth graders are not generally pampered winners, the school has also different ways of telling the universities who is who. Students with a decent grade point average are put on Honor Roll. The ones excelling in academic subjects are candidates for the California Scholarship Federation (CSF). In order to bring that point home, there is a luncheon held where the corresponding certificates are handed over, with teachers and parents invited as well.

Mom is all in tears as Airin and Ann are getting their mentions. All eyes are on her.

"Airin's last name is not V., though."

"I think she is an exchange student living with the V.s."

Ann is one of the very few students being additionally awarded lifelong membership in the CSF. That is as good as you can get.

The system is designed to stir the ambition of all undergraduates, as they watch this procedure year by year. They follow this incentive as good as they can, avoiding by all means becoming a drop-out. If they make it to the end of class twelve, they, too, will attend a spectacular ball at a country club, clad in dinner jackets and long formal dresses, the promenade to the sound of festive music included.

Mr. Parker does everything in his power to persuade us to go on to college. Even if it is to study for two years only and get a diploma in hair dressing or any other craft, he evokes all the advantages this will grant us. For example, he implies, we will be "a good credit risk" for the banks and credit cards for us would be issued at a wink. This sounds good, even better than the perspective of receiving our diplomas at the stadium, with the rest of Azusa looking on and applauding.

All parents, relatives, friends, fellow students and teachers (well – might as well do without those) would be watching us march into the stadium, clad in long gowns and becoming caps, square with the cord dangling down coquettishly. The principal would hand us our diplomas, proud as a peacock. For every single graduate, there would be applause. Most of us would cry with relief and pride at the same time.

From the very beginning of the year, I had known that I would return to my home country and complete my secondary education there. Had I known at that time, how much persuasion on the side of my old teachers would be necessary and how much bureaucracy would be involved in order to convince the State Department of Education to allow me back into my old class (and not downgrade me because they had exactly in that year changed the beginning of school from Easter to fall), I think I would have opted for California right then.

Once back home, I was first admitted on probation for three months, after which there would be exams in some crucial subjects, among them Physics. The punishment was blatantly obvious: Who do you think you are to stroll around abroad for a year and then shortly afterwards expect us to award you our valuable Abitur certificate, the best high school diploma imaginable.

The irony of fate wanted it that one year after that, when I applied to a college abroad with my German high school diploma, it was not recognized as a serious document, since it was a meek sheet of paper, headed Testimony of Maturity, listing the grades I received in all subjects. It did bear stamp and signature, but looked not half as impressive as my Azusa High School diploma which did the trick.

Chapter 25

Change is everywhere

Meanwhile, my letters home are full of Anglicisms. "Ich hatte einen großartigen Tag dort" is definitely not idiomatically correct in German. I am looking at it with a mixture of disbelief and dismay. Can I myself possibly have written this in May 1966?

During the last fifty years, German has admittedly become Americanized, if you want to call it that, but not everything introduced by the media has become standard.

Like "Thanks for the moment" in German means "What a nice moment you made me experience" and not, like it does in English, stand for "That was it for now." The expression "absolut" though, has been used successfully in German for "I agree", the way it is used in English. In spite of mocking these expressions as New German, more and more people make use of them. This even goes as far as changing grammatical sentence order.

Forerunners were the media, fashion people and aviation. One should also not underestimate the snob value of using foreign expressions, not only in Europe. While the average citizen not really pays any attention, in business and especially in advertisement people are liable to impress with the latest fad. Advertisement has long become a branch of psychology, only designed to increase sale, especially luring young people into spending their money. Teens are very susceptible to everything fashionable, cool and must have.

Who would have thought fifty years ago that German restaurants would offer a lunch special instead of Tagesessen? Even more common are nowadays mixed and creole expressions like BahnCard or Schönes-Wochenende-Tickets.

Different interest groups are reacting in different ways to this trend, that goes without mentioning. Conservative advocates of the preservation of language are nowadays called philistines or ultra-rightists. Actually, most linguists will agree in calling language change natural and unavoidable. I personally find most interesting what expression will stay and which ones disappear again.

Our AFS-group agrees on many things: The greatest music group are "The Mamas & The Papas", our favorite TV soap is "The Man from U.N.C.L.E" and the best country singer is Johnny Cash. At the end of our exchange year, all of us are kind of reluctant when asked to easily switch to our home language. During all this time, we had neither electronic contact (there was none yet) nor telephone calls (too expensive) home.

This apparently was enough to almost completely integrate or better: assimilate us 16- to 18-year-olds. More than anyone else, the Hispanic students keep on praising the advantages of the American way of life. The Europeans admit meekly to the laboriousness, bureaucracy and comparative backwardness of their countries of origin.

In order to illustrate in one example how one single year had been sufficient to turn us into little Americans, I recall how reluctantly the German AFSers tried to talk in German together near the end of our exchange. We sounded like a parody.

Ute is rolling on the floor and the rest of us with her when she mocks how we were grocery shopping back in Germany.

"I would like a box of matches and three apples", she is neighing like a horse.

"Don't pick the apples by yourself, we salespeople, too, have to buy them as we get them!" she then proceeds to chucklingly imitate the response of the shop assistant and goes on:

"We are closing now. - Imagine, they close at 6 p.m. and they were closed for two hours during lunch time and on Saturdays, they pull down the blind as soon as 2 p.m."

No wonder, I suddenly realize, working women in Germany have almost no change for shopping.

Nevertheless, even out West in California, the Sixties were an era when the business world was still dominated largely by men. Most married women are housewives with sometimes a temporary job or being engaged in some type of volunteer work. I am desperately searching for arguments in favor of my far away Europe.

"Look, the Americans cook mostly ready-made convenience foods. They don't taste as good as homemade meals made from scratch. And their kids go to school all day and even during holidays, their parents try to get rid of them, too, by sending them to camp."

Objections come up immediately:

"Oh yeah? And what is wrong with a woman trying to keep her chores manageable while her kids are taken good care of?"

In response, I repeat from hearsay: " A mother is always the best company for her children."

"This would only be true if all women were professional educators. Or destined to be handmaids for every occasion."

Feminism is already knocking on the door behind which young intellectuals of the Western world are getting ready for the future.

By and by, our discussion is gaining fieriness and America is winning clearly, when most of us girls opt for putting on make-up and criticize the fact that people in their home countries would call this stupidly vain or frivolous.

The boys state how much they will miss their daily sport lessons. However, general issues like the huge agricultural areas up in Northern California are subject to criticism. The country is quite dry and irrigated by means of long aqueducts, although even then people knew of the dangers of wasting water and also lavishing pesticides. Compared to the yield of characteristically small patches of fields in Europe, though, they harvest huge amounts of cereals and fruits.

Finally, we are touching upon a topic for everyone: food. Corn, oranges, grapes and more are getting straight A's, while nobody seems to care for the soft white slices of bread.

"Maybe the toasted variation."

"Yeah."

"Listen, guys, aren't you looking forward to short distances, public transportation and getting around easily without a car?"

"Nein, ich will as soon as possible mein own car und independent sein. Mein Vater ist Politiker. He wrote to me, dass es in der nächsten Legislaturperiode für über 16Jährige ein Schülergehalt von 30 DM per person gibt."

"You are kidding."

"No way. Besides, the Americans have no culture. And their schools are, compared to our Gymnasium, only mediocre." - "???"

We are torn in between the two systems, realizing how much we must have changed during the last few months.

Chapter 26

That was it, Class of '66

The last week of school is simply phantastic for us Seniors. After having completed all check-out formalities on Monday, the Tuesday following is Senior Ditch Day".

Instead of going to school, we are driven to the beach by bus. All the teachers are with us, too. During this excursion, they are being mobbed and vexed in a way that borders on harassment.

Anyway, teacher or not, in California teasing people has many odd forms. It is, for instance, considered a big compliment to toilet-paper a popular person's car. This means shrouding it in toilet paper overnight which is very hard to remove the next day, because the morning dew has made it cling to the lacquer.

At the beach, first thing we do is storming the children's playground, sliding, swinging and seesawing, until all the mothers and their kids leave the place to us. Too bad, they lose. And who cares when they resign and tell their kids loudly:

"Darling, forget it, let the big kids play for a change."

The whole program has been planned well. the teachers set up the BBQ and serve us as well. There is lots of coke, but no alcohol, not even beer.

Another strange custom is waiting now for some unsuspecting innocent class mates. Like at the pool, at the beach people are grabbed by a group of usually three or four and thrown in full gear into the water. For this purpose, the actors of the scene get themselves a big blanket, wrap it in no time around their victim, caught unawares and send him or mostly her flying into the waves, preferably all dressed.

The procedure is, as you may have guessed, accompanied by cries, yells and applause. But the person "honored" in this way just grins and bears it. I just manage to hand my wrist watch over to Ann before I surrender. Well, see above, after all it is considered a great compliment, what they are doing to you, a signal for popularity and liking.

The procedure has left me wet to the bones with my dress clinging to my body. While I am stalking back out of the water awkwardly, raucous comments concerning my underwear contribute to the general amusement. Yet what really gets at me, is the endless laughter and hooters.

I don't have any dry clothes with me, so I soon start to get cold. "Merciful" classmates lend me their own clothes. Dave who is six feet tall, gives me his windbreaker, which is all Azusa blue and sports a white floral pattern. Mario has some yellow-red-bluish checkered Bermuda shorts with him, better than nothing. Meanwhile, Ann is taking care of my wet clothes and shoes.

Although my hair is in a mess and I do look very strange, back in the bus on our way home I suddenly feel enthusiastically high and soon join some of my cocky classmates in throwing marshmallows all over the bus which are then picked up by and eaten among hilarious laughter.

The aisle of the bus is full of dancing and swaying youngsters. When others get up, they just push anyone in their way back into their seats. Music is blazing from portable radios.

Thinking now back of the incident, the noise must have been almost unbearable for the teachers and the bus driver.

The hype about the commencement ceremony in the football stadium had begun weeks before. With excitement mounting, the Seniors put all their efforts into getting the requirements for graduation all straight. No more mistakes afforded now! We need at least try and finally obtain all required credit points, or else! Finish our last papers, beg the teachers for the chance to give an additional presentation, thus earning some extra credit. We are thinking of different convincing arguments that might come in handy. Pity scam could do the trick, right?

Won't it be cool when all parents, relatives, friends, fellow students and teachers (oh well, them, too) get up at the sound of the school band and watch us marching into the stadium, clad in our festive gowns with the matching caps on our heads? One by one, we would receive our diplomas from the hand of our proud principal.

As the last days preceding the big event are drawing near, the students start to bet who was going to cry when being handed the diploma.

Just imagine, floodlights in the arena would turn the night into day. We would enter two by two, from the very top of the stadium, down all the stairs. The girls would wear white, the boys Aztec blue. More and more people would cheer and clap. The national anthem would sound, signaling the beginning of the program. Greeting addresses and speeches would follow. A song, a prayer and here we go – one by one, hearing our full names announced over the microphone.

When Peter comes to pick me up on the big day, he is simply dressed to kill. He is wearing the navy-blue jacket with the emblem of his military academy, combined with light grey woolen slacks and flawlessly polished black shoes. Gallantly, he assists me when I am getting into my white gown and puts the cap on my head. The way it looked with the top down, he must have cleaned his car for hours. He drives his car down the streets at an almost ceremoniously slow speed. People stop to watch. They put their heads together as they applaud. Peter is grinning from ear to ear. I busy myself putting my cap into the right place.

"Miss Christine Marie Guernsey, Mister Alfred Peter Stone, Miss Irene Schlor…"

I seem to be the only one with no middle name. But when our principal calls my name, mindful to pronounce it correctly, the clapping even increases for a moment.

When everyone finally is equipped with the satin-lined folders, in which there is a slip of paper promising its upcoming replacement with the real thing, we march back down into the stadium to the music of our band. Now it is time for the "round of honor", flanked by our applauding teachers. Then, finally, refreshments and home-made cookies with our visitors on the lawn.

Our proud parents congratulate us formally and let their polaroid cameras click. Hugs are allowed by the rules agreed: Bodies only touch above the waist; hands clap lightly on shoulders or backs.

Rob Beverly's mother comes towards me and discreetly slips a piece of tissue into my hand – thank God! She introduces me to all her relatives and Rob marvels at seeing me in his mother's arms. He starts to scratch his ear and seems even more puzzled to see me cry.

"Why are you crying, hm?" He asks me embarrassedly.

"I don't know, I am so happy and sad. It's good-bye forever."

Yet there seems to be no end to tearful talks.

The teachers make a point in talking to every single student of theirs, as much as they can.

"I liked your classes the best" I sob in Mr. Parker's direction.

Very seriously articulating every word, he answers:

"You must write us, Irene! How can we otherwise know what those politicians in Europe are up to?"

After having turned in my gown, Peter and I rush towards his car to fetch my casual clothes and shoes, because now the fun part is supposed to start. We are heading for a bowling alley to attend the "Senior All-nighter".

The place is rented and closed for us exclusively. The bowling area, the food counters, the recreation corners with their benches and tables, the dancing floor – all reserved for Azusa High School Seniors. Live-Music elates our already bitchin' mood. Bitchin' is cooler than cool, and also a no-go expression for good girls.

But actually, the greatest feeling of all is the realization of having accomplished something substantial plus, we all rejoice at the prospect of having to do no homework whatsoever for the months to come. Last not least, we are filled with the pride of having become adults now.

Being good in sports, Peter soon becomes the star of the dancing floor, dancing the "Watutsi", "Frog" and "Mashed Potatoes".

At four in the morning, there is breakfast.

We are loudly protesting being asked to leave about an hour later. How can they be so cruel! It has been a ball, though.

Chapter 27

From Coast to Coast

For two weeks we are touring the States from California way up to Canada to the Niagara Falls and back to New York and finally Washington, D.C. Our bus is very comfortable and airconditioned - a feature we definitely need because we spend about five hours a day on it.

Every afternoon we stop in a different state, met by the local big shots, more often than not with the red carpet rolled out. We stay at host families who receive us very friendly, trying to please us and be of help wherever needed. This includes even cleaning service for our clothes as well as a shoulder for psychological problems. We have our meals with them and get a lunch bag for the next day on top of it.

The days are filled with impressive local highlights and how do we appreciate it, let alone feel grateful? Once on the bus, we start to criticize everything thoughtlessly and cruelly the teenage way, I must admit.

"They call it The Chicken Ride" is Susi's comment, when we find almost the same food in our lunch bags for two days in a row.

Scottsdale, Arizona, has left a very lasting impression with me, probably partly because it was our first stop. The dry heat of ending June embraced us vigorously upon leaving the bus. The immediate start of the professionally prepared welcome speech left us stunned. It was the mayor of the town who greeted us, correctly dressed in a dark suit, white shirt and tie, mind you. This scenario was to became a Deja Vue in the days ahead.

The topic would be understanding among different nations, about getting to know people as the key to finding together and, needless to say, the leading role of the US as a Goodwill Promoter.

As it was customary in those days, the girls wore dresses only and the boys had slacks and shirts on. Our thoughts were fixed on the air conditioning which hopefully would be awaiting us in the cars. But we politely applauded and cheered like professionals as well. Since if we had been receptive to anything taught to us, it was to being young ambassadors of our respective countries. An envoi never commits the faux-pas of not smiling or worse, disapproving.

The press people clicked their cameras, after which they swarmed out to quickly pick among us the victims of their choice.

"Where are you from? How was your year in America? Do you like Arizona?"

Eager host families met us then and away we drove. Never shall I forget the physical shock I felt when entering an ice-cold car after having been outside in the burning heat.

"The temperature is only around 100° F, in July it easily gets up to 120° F."

All around us, there really seems to be only dessert of a yellow-brownish color. Again, I am getting this feeling of respect for the American spirit that is determined to make the best out of every situation. Roll up your sleeves and get at it.

The next day in Silver City, New Mexico (nomen est omen) we get to see an open pit mine. It is one of our best stops on this trip, due to quite a bit of walking and a very professional guided tour. I get to stay with a doctor's family and I remember looking fascinatedly at the super short cropped hair and fingernails of the master of the house. He willingly explains to me at length the correlation between lack of hygiene and illness. I am impressed.

When the time comes for a stop in Big Spring, Texas, we are getting briefed in a different way. We sing the song of "A yellow rose in Texas". Everything seems a number bigger. The major and the city council assembled, teachers, parents AFS people have lined up to welcome us, applauding enthusiastically.

The first event after arrival is a real Rodeo which most girls cannot find anything in, since it is nothing but one cowboy after the other getting on a wild and scary bull and being thrown off immediately. The boys among us, though, are besides themselves with emotion uttering sounds that perfectly mix with the blaring country music.

The following barbeque, its grill, the steaks – everything is bigger, larger, in short, of a size never before witnessed. Different from California, almost every man here in Texas is dressed like a full-fledged cowboy.

Moreover, they don't look like they got dressed up for us especially. It fits as if it was their regular outfit. Everyone looks authentic in his large hat, the silver kerchief chain with the turquoise gemstone around the neck, the checkered shirt, leather slip covers over the jeans and – last not least – the characteristic cowboy boots, more often than not in tobacco brown, pointed, with a loop to fix the spur.

And sure enough, a square dance show is rounding up the perfect "Bonanza" effect.

Shawnee, Oklahoma, is the disillusionment following. It becomes obvious right away that people there are poor. Nevertheless, they are trying very hard to keep up appearances. But the depressing effect on us pulls us down and we are back to reality. The verandas of the houses we stay at look like they once must have had a coat of white paint. In the backyard there is no grass, just the bare earth. Aimlessly picking chicken, a sagging clothesline at the side and the repeated clatter of the insect screen just heighten the impression of dreariness.

The daughter of the family I am staying with is my age. Practically on arrival, she gives me a long thorough lecture on teenage pregnancy, also touching upon the dangers of abortion and – sure enough – abandoned children. My being shocked is only partly due to the content of what she is talking about, but I also need to concentrate hard to understand her acoustically. Only the day before I had laughed my head off at the amiably different accent of the Texans, but this one was really tough at the beginning. My spontaneous reaction is one of dismay instead of empathy and I suddenly start to cry in spite of myself.

The next morning, my co-travelers tell me similar stories. Are we already too much pampered and egoistic to be able to bear a disturbing thought?

Liberty, Missouri, then Tremont, Illinois, are the beginning of deja-vue. However, the excursion into Pennsylvania Dutch Country gives us the impression of being catapulted into the 19th century or, alternately, into the middle of a movie shooting. But this is real life, no cameras, no assistant to the director, no make-up artists. We can see horse drawn carriages, people in old-fashioned dress, plough and oxen in the fields.

When the bus stops, our chaperones, Janet and Linda, encourage us to address the people in German. The friendly reaction we get is amazing: we had been understood and even get the gist of their responses, but we are unable to define or assign to any specific language what we hear.

No, they have no machines, no electricity, no button on their clothing. They reject military service or anything that reminds one of it, like competition or even efficiency. They are called the "the Amish" and the government grants them to have their own way on this stretch of land.

We tend to find rather conservative-religiously oriented host families. The girls have their hair in braids and wear aprons, the women wear their coiffure in a tight knot and are dressed old-fashioned. In our lunch bag the next day we find quotes from the Bible aside good food.

We are gradually getting a feeling of being overfed, unable to consume more new places.

One factor to fortify that feeling is the visit to a sausage factory, which is obviously the pride of its owner and the whole town. He must have also been the sponsor of our stay.

There is a sort of assembly line we follow all the way, that is: from the pig to the product. In the beginning we watch the piggies being cleaned from several nozzles splashing water over them. Squeaking, they mount the running band one after the other. They almost look cute, being shoveled alongside us, so pink and clean. But the next thing we see is electric shock buffers coming down precisely aimed at their heads. The animals flinch and wince, then they collapse. We actually get to witness every single step of the process. As a reward, we are finally given each one pair of sausages.

Our enthusiasm and genuine interest are only being revived at the gigantic Niagara Falls in Canada. Having crossed the national border with special one-day passes, we are confronted with one of the highlights of our trip. Nobody prepared us for what a great impression these waterfalls would leave on us. It isn't only the unbelievable amounts of water endlessly thundering down into an invisible abyss, it is the spray and spume surrounding us, while the ear-deafening sound of the water mutes every attempt at a conversation. A sense of respect and awe before the force of nature is making the round.

Towards the end, we spend what felt like a day on a ferry taking us all around the city of New York. The Statue of Liberty seems to wave us good-bye and another walk through the urban canyons promises adventure, while just one year ago we had been afraid to roam them.

The last stop is Washington, D.C., where all AFS busses meet for a big farewell. A picnic lunch on the lawn of the White House comes under the familiar slogan "Walk together, talk together, all ye peoples of the earth! Then and only then shall ye have peace!"

We try to meet as many different fellow students as possible with everybody sharing the same opinion: One year was not enough. We would have loved to stay on.

Chapter 28

I travelled the world on MS Seven Seas

All European AFSers who had entered the US by plane via Frankfurt are now shipped back to Rotterdam via New York. There is something special to this trip as well: It will be the last journey of the SS Seven Seas, which will therefrom never sail again.

We shall be aboard for eleven days. Except for daily cruises on Lake Constance, I have never been aboard a ship before. I really wonder how so much wood can be staying on the water without sinking. Unbelievable! But once we are on board, it sure will sink. Only think of the long railway with its hand lead of iron – it will surely slip to the side and all of us will fall right into the water. How can a few thick ropes tied to pegs keep the ship from moving on? When we come aboard with our heavy luggage in hand, we can hear the ropes grind. We were allowed to ship only one package each, the rest of our belongings are right with us.

"Raise your legs, gal!" I hear a sailor shouting when Christine almost staggers over the bord tie.

Puzzled, Christine looks at him and I look at Christine.

"Long time no sees!" I shriek at her like a native American, throwing my arms around her neck. Christine is my old classmate from Heilbronn. She had been allocated to Alabama and we hadn't been in contact for a year.

Dropping our luggage, we impede the whole traffic line.

"Move on, don't stop! Over there at the desk you will get your cabin numbers. Don't stop here!"

"See you later, alligator!" I fool around.

"In a while, crocodile!" she clowns back.

The language used on bord is exclusively German, to make that clear from the beginning. The crew and our chaperones speak only in German to us. But we cannot cut with a knife our English which we had been using for the longest time, it seems to us. The force imposed upon us makes us rebel.

Why should we switch to German right now? We will be speaking enough of it once we are back home.

Thinking back now, I am sure we couldn't have easily switched to German without these vital eleven days of re-education on board.

In the cabin I am allocated there are four bunk beds. We four German girls have almost no space to even turn around. through the porthole we can see lots of water and part of the New York skyline. As fast as we can, we rush back on deck to watch our ship cast off. Some of the host families living nearby had come to wave us good-bye.

Naturally, the Californias and other far away families had not come, though almost everyone had sent a telegram to bide farewell to their leaving sons and daughter of one year.

It must have been a grotesque sight: Gesticulating, yelling loudly and running back and forth, where possible, many of us tried to make out one of the faces below us, there at the kay.

The fact that almost every one of us was yelling "Mom", didn't help much either.

A band of white clad sailors is playing happy tunes, the ropes are being released one by one, the siren blasts out three long sounds.

"Full speed ahead!"

As the skyline fades, we retreat to our cabins to get ready for dinner.

Funniest thing, the table cloth is moist, almost wet. Otherwise, the plates might slip off, get it? There is nothing else to mock about, absolutely nothing. The layout of the dishes and cutlery is appetizing, the dining hall smells inviting.

"Fried potatoes with lard!" I can hear Ludolf jubilate. Ludolf is from East Frisia and my mate from bus # 13.

The food is very good and more and more of us realize what we had been missing and what a feast it was to have it back.

To sum it up, our trip back as well as the whole one-year stay had been organized perfectly. Even now, we are all involved in a program on board which captures our attention without giving us the feeling of restriction. Having been conditioned to oblige, we are happy with the rules and, believe it or not, from the third day on bord onward, most of us returnees make use of German more than of English.

In the evenings, our cabin crew usually sits on the narrow beds and we are talking endlessly; German, English, whatever comes to our minds first. My three roommates all have different perfumes with them and we shower the cabin with an orgy of scents. The bathroom is down the aisle.

Talking about bathrooms, during this journey I took part in a crash course in nautical terminology and now cannot resist the temptation to mention a curious fact I then learned about.

Well then, besides the better-known expressions like starboard, backboards, bells and so on, there is the so-called Allemansend, a frayed rope which hangs down into the water near backboard. It is supposedly used instead of toilet paper. I confess to never having actually seen it, though I immediately understood what it meant, since it reminded me of the latrines of the Romans. In the Roman cities, there were public toilets where citizens sat in a row, relieving themselves side by side. There were sponges on sticks which hung in vessels filled with diluted vinegar. People would pass them to each other for cleaning themselves.

In our cabin, while the moon is shining through the porthole, Regine confesses that her aim is to become a cheerleader at Borussia Dortmund Football Club. There weren't any yet, that was true, but she was going to introduce that custom. She sounds determined about it.

As to Jutta, she vows to go back to the States as soon as she has her German high school diploma, the Abitur. Her host family would help her to make a new start over there.

Sylvia aims at a career with the UNO in New York. "You can earn tons of money at that job!"

And me? After the lights are out, I come to think more and more of my own family back in Germany. I cannot wait to see them again. And I am dying to see all my classmates again. Just imagine all the stories I would tell them! My best friend Monika and her family were actually waiting for me in Rotterdam harbor. A sister of hers had spent the summer in a camp in France and now her parents had set out to pick up the two of us.

As much as I try to forget him, I cannot help but also think of Kemal, the good-looking Turkish boy whom I had fallen in love with during our bus trip across the States.

"I will come to Germany and I will marry you!" he had whispered into My next aim was to finish high school in my home town, then followed by a college education in order to become a school teacher, preferably at the University of Tübingen. Since my English had become so fluent now, I would easily manage that in no time.

Never ever would I then have believed anyone who told me I was going to attend Robert College in Istanbul.